I0670264

THEY ALL
HAD A

THEY ALL
HAD A

SECRET

MICHELE LEATHERS

sourcebooks
fire

Copyright © 2026 by Michele Leathers
Cover and internal design © 2026 by Sourcebooks
Cover design by Casey Moses
Cover image © Jane Morley/Trevillion Images, Vector-
World/Shutterstock, bdvect 1/Shutterstock
Internal design by Tara Jaggers/Sourcebooks

Sourcebooks and the colophon are registered trademarks of Sourcebooks.

All rights reserved. No part of this book may be reproduced in any form or by
any electronic or mechanical means, including information storage and retrieval
systems—except in the case of brief quotations embodied in critical articles or
reviews—without permission in writing from its publisher, Sourcebooks.

No part of this book may be used or reproduced in any manner for the
purpose of training artificial intelligence technologies or systems.

The characters and events portrayed in this book are fictitious or
are used fictitiously. Any similarity to real persons, living or dead,
is purely coincidental and not intended by the author.

Published by Sourcebooks Fire, an imprint of Sourcebooks
1935 Brookdale RD, Naperville, IL 60563–2773
(630) 961-3900
sourcebooks.com

Originally self-published as *They All Had a Secret* in 2021 by Michele Leathers.

Cataloging-in-Publication Data is on file with the Library of Congress.

Printed and bound in the United States of America.
PAH 10 9 8 7 6 5 4 3 2 1

For Joey, Jacob & Morgan:

PROLOGUE

True crime junkies, it is time once again to untangle the twisted truth. I'm your host, Cam Whitmeyer, and this is my podcast, *Unsolved, Unfinished: Criminals on the Run*. This week, we dive even deeper into the Bellany Silverfield and Quentin Colson case. Welcome to episode two, "A Friend and a Frenemy."

In order to bring you this week's episode, I traveled to Smithfield, North Carolina, a small town that garnered national attention over the horrific crime and scandal. Bellany Silverfield and Quentin Colson were two popular high school students who seemed to have it all—beauty, brains, athletic success, and bright futures ahead of them. But everything changed on the night of Bellany's seventeenth birthday. Friends, family, and the authorities are still wondering what happened to Bellany and Quentin. Where did they go? If they're still out there somewhere, will they kill again?

During my visit to Smithfield, I had the opportunity to speak to a couple of Bellany and Quentin's friends.

Sandra Sanders and Bellany were on their high school cheerleading squad together for two years.

"That's right, Bellany and I were best friends. Practically everybody at school idolized her. Quentin was super focused on basketball—to a fault. I swear, that's all he ever wanted to talk about. They were the perfect couple. I'm still shocked."

Vivy Bailey, a classmate and close friend of Quentin's, shared a very different perspective.

"Bellany was a mean girl, plain and simple. A bully. She manipulated Quentin all the time. I'll tell you what I want to know, Cam. I want to know where they are. Somebody has to have seen them. Open your eyes, people! They killed someone. An innocent girl named Constance Perry. Justice for Constance!"

Justice for Constance is something many Smithfield residents agree on. In spite of being a relative stranger in this small town, her shocking murder has shaken the community.

I'll be traveling to Virginia next week to speak with Jack Masnon, Constance's older brother. I'll share that interview with you on the next episode of *Unsolved, Unfinished: Criminals on the Run*. Stay tuned.

CHAPTER 1

CHARITY (BELLANY)

Veronica is clueless. *Do I look like a lowlife housekeeper?* As the owner, she should know the front desk is where the eye candy is supposed to be. That's where I belong. I don't care if she's providing me with a free hotel room to live in. What kind of consolation is that? I wanted to smack her in the face. This job is insulting, and she acts like she's doing me some huge favor. She has no idea what I'm capable of.

Forest-green carpet, wood-paneled walls, pictures of wildlife, a chandelier with fake candles—all intended to make hotel guests feel like they are staying in a log cabin. To me, it just looks like an old lady's bedroom. The green plaid bedspread, which matches the carpet, is perfectly smoothed out and exactly centered over the mattress, ready for the next hotel guest who will never know that the sheet underneath isn't clean. All I did was spray it with Febreze.

I turn on the vacuum, push it across the carpet a couple times, then leave it running idle. That's enough. It's time for a break. I turn on the TV, pull up a chair, and try to ignore the hum of the vacuum in the background.

One minute later and the vacuum is already annoying me. I turn the volume up on the TV. Oh good, a catfight is starting between two housewives. The villain is going to win, I'm sure of it. Yep. I ascribe to Darwin's philosophy of natural selection; the strong evolve and survive. I'm one of the strong ones.

Sitting on the dresser next to the TV is a dusty assortment of flyers and pamphlets for local Chehalis, Washington, attractions. One of them is for a mall called Yard Birds. I've driven past the building. I heard it shut down years ago after people started shopping online.

My attention shifts to the dirty towels piled on top of the cleaning cart. When I was around eight years old, I remember stuffing my clean clothes under my bed or dumping them back in the laundry basket so I wouldn't have to put them away. As a result, my clothes were usually wrinkled. But I didn't care. I was just a kid.

My dad would get mad at my mom, because I looked a mess. Then my mom would get mad at me, because my wrinkled clothes weren't her fault—at least in her opinion. She could have put the clothes away herself and solved the whole problem, but she didn't. She insisted that I do it. Only, I didn't want to. I wanted to play and have fun, like most kids that age. But she never let up on her demands, preferring to punish me for the slightest little things, especially for not putting away my clothes correctly.

Her punishments included springing demands on me at the most inconvenient times. I know she did it on purpose—she was vicious and calculating that way. I think she truly enjoyed making me miserable, ruining my plans, deliberately trying to snatch any and all happiness away from me.

She was unhappy herself, and she wanted me to be miserable just like her—a true gem of a mother.

I would say things to my mom like, *I'm going to go play outside*, and she'd say, *Not until you clean your bedroom and the bathroom first, Bellany*. I'd say, *I'm going across the street to the park*, and she'd say, *Take out the garbage, stack the dishwasher, and wipe down the kitchen table first, Bellany*.

My mom never made my twin brother, Bridger, do any cleaning. He was her favorite child and could do no wrong.

One day I finally got fed up and said, *You love Bridger more than me*. I wanted her to tell me that she loved us both the same, but she didn't say anything. She didn't tell me I was wrong. She didn't say that she loved me. I guess I already knew it was true, but it was still a gut punch when she admitted it with her silence. In my mind, I could hear her saying, *I hate you, Bellany, and wish you had never been born*.

So I lost my temper and started yelling at her. I didn't say the things that were really bothering me deep down inside, like how rejected I felt. I stuck to surface stuff. I guess I did this so she wouldn't know how hurt I really was. I said things like, *Why doesn't Bridger ever have to do anything? Why does he get to sit on the couch and play video games all day? Why do I have to clean everything?*

Then my mom had the nerve to tell me that boys have other jobs to do like yard work and mowing the grass. What a joke. First off, Bridger never mowed anything. We had a hired landscaper do all of the yard work. And why couldn't boys clean the house? Why only girls? She had such a warped perspective, and I was tired of it.

That was the day I decided to make messes instead of clean, and I stopped doing what my mom asked me to do. I'd leave the milk out on the counter to spoil, spill soda then let it dry and get everybody's shoes sticky. I would drop food onto the couch. I didn't care.

My mom would say things like, *Get in there and clean that up, you ungrateful little…* Fill in the blank. She would add all kinds of vicious names and curse words. But I held my ground. I was not going to do anything she asked me to do.

She would get out a wooden spoon and threaten me with it. I still didn't comply, so she'd hit me. And yes, it left a mark every time, but I never gave in. I put up with the bruises until I ultimately got what I wanted.

My dad was so fed up with coming home to a messy house that he hired a housekeeper. My mom should have thanked me. Instead, she held a grudge that continued to get worse the older I got.

When I was finally big enough to wrestle the wooden spoon away from her, she tried a different tactic. She broke down in front of me sobbing and begging me to stop fighting with her, telling me she wanted us to start over and have a real relationship. I began to think that maybe the reason she treated me the way she did was my fault. I started going out of my way to be nicer, believing that if I tried hard enough she might be able to love me.

That's when she hurt me the deepest. She never left another bruise on my skin, but she tore me up on the inside. She started acting like I didn't exist. She literally stopped talking to me and stopped looking at me. She erased me from her life. It was like as soon as she saw me opening up and trying, she sprung her trap to inflict as much emotional damage as possible at my most vulnerable moment.

After that, my mom went overboard, pouring her attention onto Bridger. She doted on him to the extreme, constantly. She'd take him out to eat and to the movies, and they'd go shopping together. They shared private conversations and inside jokes right in front of me. It was cruel and deliberate, and it hurt.

How could a mom do that to her only daughter? She had me second-guessing myself until I realized it was all just a mind game. I vowed to never let her hurt me again. I learned how to lock down the vulnerable parts of myself. I became completely immune.

A commercial break flashes up on the TV screen, ripping me from my thoughts. My show is already over. I force myself to get up out of the chair, groaning in frustration, then I flip the switch on the vacuum to turn it off. The room is so much quieter now, but it's not peaceful. I still have to finish cleaning.

This is so disgusting. Why can't people be more considerate and at least clean their own hair out of the shower drain? I bend down with a gloved hand and a wad of toilet paper to grab it. I tug. A thick clump comes free. Wait, that's not just hair. My stomach churns. Is that…poop?

Don't get sick, don't get sick, I tell myself repeatedly, as I toss the poop-hair and my gloves into the trash sack. I scrub my hands thoroughly in the sink, eyes watering, bile rising in my throat. Then I run out of the bathroom. I'm pacing back and forth, trying to settle my stomach back down, taking deep breaths. But it's not helping.

I burst through the door and out into the hallway, where I'm surrounded by gray walls, a mirror image of the ever-present overcast sky outside. I pass by hotel room door after hotel room door. Each time their bright orange color makes my eyes water even more. My gaze lowers to the floor, which is covered in brown carpet, reminding me of that disgusting thing I pulled from the drain. My stomach churns again, and I take off running for the exit.

The cold air outside seems to help. After a few minutes, I can finally relax my breathing and my stomach settles.

A bird flies overhead in the direction of Veronica's house. Ever since the first time I saw that magnificent home, I wanted it for myself—the angled roof, the intricate detail on the stained glass windows, the balconies and the massive oak front door. Every bit of it is perfect.

The hotel, however, is not perfect. But it has potential. The exterior doesn't share any cheesy log cabin decor. It's a large single-story building with plain beige siding and a dark shingled roof. It sits on one of the mountain hilltops, surrounded by tall fir trees. The only notable feature is a large, covered entrance with simple wooden posts. It's essentially a blank canvas.

The house, the hotel, the campground, and this secluded location up on the mountain… This is why I'm here. This is why I stayed in Chehalis. I am going to take it all away from Veronica. I'm going to take her grandson, Roy, too. He's already falling under my spell. It's just a matter of time before he can't live without me.

I always take what I want. If you can get it, then you deserve it. Survival of the fittest. The strong end up on top. That's just the way it is in life. Some are winners and some are losers. I am a winner.

I return to the room once again, furious with the nasty lowlife who defecated in the shower. I'd make him clean the toilet with his toothbrush and then brush his teeth with it if he were here.

Before I leave the room, I place a couple of mints on the pillows and keep one for myself to get rid of the gross taste in my mouth. I push the vacuum and the cleaning cart out into the hallway.

Ugh. Those orange doors. When this hotel becomes mine, I'll change everything: the color scheme, the furniture, the landscaping outside, the light fixtures, the signage. This place will be unrecognizable. It will look like a palace.

After I finish cleaning another hotel room, I put away the supplies and head to the lobby with a fake smile on my face, ready to see Veronica.

She looks up from her romance novel and smiles at me, or is she laughing? I bet she thinks it's funny that someone as attractive and elegant as me has to do this kind of work.

A small oscillating fan blows onto her wrinkled face. Wisps of her salt-and-pepper hair flutter in the breeze. "All done?" she asks. "Any problems?"

Be polite, I tell myself. "No problems. Everything's fine," I reply with a practiced smile.

"How bad was room 102?"

Room 102 was the poop room. Did she already know? I study her face, looking for signs of deception. She seems way too eager to hear my answer. She's leaning forward in her chair, one eyebrow arched. Yeah. I think she knew exactly what was waiting for me. I won't give her the satisfaction. "All of the rooms were about the same today," I say with a shrug. "Nothing all that unusual."

She places a bookmark between the pages of her book and sets it down on a stack of about six others. "You never complain, you're on time for work, you're efficient and reliable. As far as I'm concerned, Charity, you can stay here forever."

Don't worry. I plan on it.

She picks up a flyswatter and smacks a fly right on the edge of her desk, then motions for me to clean it up. I hate when she does this kind of stuff. I smile to hide my seething irritation, then grab a couple paper towels out of the storage room and a bottle of spray cleaner.

As I wipe up the fly guts, I catch Veronica staring at a framed photo on her desk. I started working for her almost a month ago and have been in this office many times but have never seen her take notice of it before. "Who's that?" I ask.

She reaches for the picture and runs her fingers over it. "This is my husband, Vance, and my daughter, Jessica. She's Roy's mother. This picture was taken about five years ago when we opened the campground." She sighs. "They've both since passed away."

Great. She's going to talk about dead people. I don't want to have to pretend to care. But I know if I don't act appropriately, Veronica will think that I'm cold-hearted and insensitive. People like her don't seem to understand that my lack of compassion has nothing to do with them. It's just who I am.

I place my hand over my heart and make a sad face. "Oh my gosh, Veronica. I'm so sorry for your loss. That must be so difficult—"

She waves a hand to stop me. "I've gotten used to them being gone."

Good. Glad to hear.

"You know, Charity, everyone misses their loved ones after they pass. The hardest part is not having someone around you can depend on."

Veronica sets down the photo and leans back in her chair, attempting to fold her short arms over her chest, but she's too fat. Her fingers barely touch. Why try to fold your arms when you know you can't do it? That makes no sense to me. It can't be relaxing for her.

The chair creaks as she leans back even further. She looks up at the ceiling. "Let's see now... Vance passed away almost two years ago, and it's been five years since Jessica passed."

Oh, we're still talking about that?

"Jessica died when Roy was thirteen. He has been living with me ever since. I can't believe he's eighteen and going to graduate soon... If only his momma could be there when he walks across the stage to receive his diploma..." She lowers her arms, which I'm sure is a relief. Then she looks at me and pauses.

Time to bring on the fake tears. "That's so sad," I say as my eyes begin to water. "Losing his mom, that must be so hard for him." I run a finger across my cheek to stop a tear from falling.

Veronica pulls me into her squishy body for a hug. She's so disgusting, so fat and gross. Her clammy skin presses against me. I hold my breath until she lets go so I don't have to breathe in her mothball smell.

She picks up one of the paper towels that I didn't use to wipe up the fly guts and hands it to me to dry my tears. "Roy misses his mother, something terrible. But he's a strong boy. He has really stepped up around here. Especially since Vance died."

"I hope you don't mind me asking, but how did they die?" I actually only want to know how Jessica died. This will be helpful information in my interactions with Roy. I'm still trying to gain his trust.

She shrugs like it isn't a big deal. "Vance smoked like a chimney. I always told him those cigarettes would kill him one day, and they did. But he lived a long life, and I know he's in a better place." Her eyes slide back to the picture on her desk. "Jessica died in a car accident. She fell asleep at the wheel."

Interesting. There might be details worth knowing. Why was she so tired? What was going on? I blot my eyes with the paper towel. "Was Roy in the car with her when it happened?"

Veronica shakes her head. "He was here at the house with me, safe and sound." She reaches into a bag of Hershey's Kisses and pulls out a handful.

She's such a pig.

"Do you have any other children?" I ask, hoping the answer is no.

People in town have told me that Roy is the sole heir to Veronica's estate. I hope that's true, otherwise my plans aren't going to be quite as simple as I thought.

"Nope. Jessica was my only one."

Good. Now the only other concern I have is Roy's father. Is he still involved in his life? Does Veronica have a good relationship with him? I guess those questions can wait for another conversation. I'm going to focus on Jessica right now.

I lean in close to the picture, studying it. Jessica's hair was dark brown, almost black, which happens to be the same color I currently dye mine. She had green eyes like mine too—well, like my contacts. My eyes are naturally blue. I wonder if Roy and Veronica think of Jessica when they look at me. Do they see the same similarities that I see? "She was so beautiful," I say, and I'm telling the truth. She really was gorgeous.

The hotel lobby door opens, and in walks a young family of three. The little girl has an ice cream cone that's dripping everywhere. I almost grumble in frustration, anticipating that I will be the one cleaning up the mess, but I stop myself quickly and smile instead.

"Welcome to Hilltop Manor. Checking in?" Veronica asks.

The girl wipes her sticky hand on a couch cushion. Hello, idiot parents. Control your child. But of course her parents aren't paying attention. They're discussing the nightly rates with Veronica.

I'm about to walk out the door when Veronica calls my name. I'm still getting used to responding to the name Charity. I turn back around. She better not ask me to clean up that ice cream mess.

"I forgot to tell you that the porch light needs a new light bulb." Veronica returns her focus to the family, not giving me an opportunity to respond.

Excuse me? I'm supposed to be done cleaning for the day. My shift is over. What is going on? Just two minutes ago we were discussing her dead husband and daughter. I even made myself cry. And now all of that's forgotten. It's back to business as usual, and I have to do something that isn't even part of my job description? Where's Roy? He usually does stuff like this.

I swear, sometimes Veronica reminds me of my mother. *Keep it up, Veronica. Yep. You just wait. You'll get what you deserve.*

I walk around to the other side of the counter, trying to fight back the anger growing inside me. It's going to take me forever to track down a ladder and a light bulb. I don't even know which porch light she's talking about.

As I continue down the hallway toward one of the storage rooms, I pass by a garbage can and spot an empty Little Debbie box stuffed inside it. No way! Veronica already ate the entire box of snack cakes? I just gave those to her a couple hours ago.

Suddenly I'm feeling much happier. In fact, I'm nearly laughing. This is too easy. She's killing herself with every bite.

When she dies, people are going to assume it was her own fault. They'll never suspect it was me.

CHAPTER 2

ROY

Wind and rain hits me in the face as I push open the door. The gust blows straight down the hallway behind me. February in Washington—always wet, always miserable. The smell of damp pine and old shingles fills the air.

I yank my hoodie tighter around my head and make a beeline for the dumpster, trash bag slapping against my leg. Before I get back to the side door, Grandma pokes her head out.

"Go check on Charity, will you? She's out front fixing that porch light. I don't want her getting shocked or slipping or something."

"I'm sure she's fine," I say.

"Will you just do it, please?"

I nod. "Yeah." Doesn't mean I want to.

I stall for a second, dragging my feet. Wind cuts between the hotel and the maintenance shed as I round the corner.

The hotel entrance has a large covered area. On one side is a porch with rocking chairs and benches. Charity's already there, standing on a stack of milk crates. She's got her hair tied up in some kind of messy bun that still somehow looks perfect.

I stop walking and just watch her for a second. I see the way she moves—focused, confident. She's got this unforgettable face. Big eyes. Full lips and straight, perfect teeth that flash when she laughs, which happens a lot. She's not just pretty—she's the prettiest girl I've ever seen. And that's a problem.

I swallow hard, worried my attraction to her is too obvious. "Need help?" I call out, finally moving closer.

She glances down at me with that lazy half-smile that makes it impossible to think straight. "Nope. I've got it."

I reach out anyway, my hands close to her waist, but not quite touching her. "Grandma sent me. She thought you might crack your head open or something."

"Sweet of her." Charity twists the bulb once, twice. It flickers, then clicks on—steady and warm, casting light across her face. Her eyes shine for a second like the glow hit them just right.

She tries to hop down, but the milk crates slip. My hands instinctively grip her waist, pulling her close. Her arms latch around my neck and I hold her against my chest. Time seems to stop while we're frozen like that, looking into each other's eyes. If I was going to kiss her, this would be the moment. My entire body is screaming at me to do it, but the voice in the back of my head is saying stop. The look in Charity's eyes tells me I have her permission, which only makes this harder.

I carefully lower her to the ground.

She steps back, slowly sliding her hands down my chest until we break contact. "Okay. That was…not graceful."

"Could've been worse," I say. I'm both relieved and kicking myself for resisting this moment.

I shove my hands in my pockets, trying not to look at Charity too long—trying to ignore the way my brain's spinning right now. The way her presence always seems to fog up every clear thought I have.

"You sure you don't have a secret death wish?" I ask, but that's not the real question on my mind. I wonder if she knows how badly I have wanted something like this, and how close I was to giving in just now.

"Death wish?" She smiles. "No, nothing like that."

Rain drips from the edge of the porch roof, landing like a curtain behind us, but it's not enough to hide what just happened. My girlfriend Samantha is supposed to arrive soon, and as guilty as I feel, I know it must look even worse.

I glance toward the driveway, wondering if I'll see her car pulling in. I don't.

Charity follows my gaze. "Your girlfriend coming soon?"

"Yep," I say, and then we're both just standing there under the light from the new bulb, the sound of rain all around us.

I know I should go inside. I *know* I should walk away. I feel so guilty thinking about what it's going to do to Samantha when she finds out that Charity lives here. That we see each other every day. That I haven't said anything. She'll be devastated. I know it. She'll think I've been hiding this from her on purpose. And maybe I have.

I don't want to be that guy—the one who lies, who cheats, who breaks the girl who trusted him. I've seen what that looks like, up close. My dad took off before I turned one. Mom said he started sleeping around while she was still pregnant with me. When she told me about it, it was like it still hurt her—like it still *defined* her. She burned every photo of him, of me as a baby too, because he was in them.

When Mom died, Grandma told me she tried to contact him, but he didn't respond. He didn't come to the funeral. He didn't even send flowers—nothing.

That kind of abandonment leaves a permanent hole. I swear, I won't be like him, but sometimes, when I'm around Charity, when my thoughts drift where they shouldn't—I wonder if I'm fooling myself.

"I didn't expect the crate to wobble like that," Charity says, brushing off her jeans.

"That's kinda why they make ladders," I say.

She laughs. It's light and warm, and it makes my chest ache in a way I wish it didn't.

I shouldn't be feeling this way about anyone but Samantha. She is my first real girlfriend, and even though we've only been dating a few months, that doesn't change the fact that I made a commitment to her. What does it say about me if I go behind her back at the first opportunity?

I take a step, about to head inside. "I'll let Grandma know you didn't fall and die."

Charity gives me that sideways smile again. "I appreciate it."

I start walking, head down, heart pounding like I just got away with something.

"Roy," a voice calls out. "What's going on?" It's Samantha. She is walking through the parking lot, headed straight toward me. Her hair and sweatshirt are damp from the rain. She folds her arms tightly across her chest, glaring at me. I realize she hasn't just arrived. She must have been sitting in the parking lot for a while—long enough to have watched everything that just happened.

Samantha used to come by the hotel every afternoon to hang out, but lately she's been busy with yearbook and prom committee responsibilities, so I haven't seen her outside of school. I should have mentioned Charity right from the start, but I never did. It's been an entire month since Grandma hired her.

"Oh, hey Samantha," I say as if I have nothing to hide.

"That's all you have to say to me?" Her eyes scan me, then Charity.

"Okay, listen. What you saw—it isn't what you think. My grandma sent me out here to help with a light bulb." I gesture to Charity. "Samantha, this is Charity. Charity, this is my girlfriend, Samantha."

"Hi, Samantha," Charity says with a smile. "Roy told me that you'd be coming over today. It's so nice to finally meet you."

Samantha raises her eyebrows, looking at me, as if waiting for me to explain.

"My grandma hired Charity to help clean. She's living in one of the hotel rooms."

"She's living here?"

I don't know what to say to her. I'm afraid anything that comes out of my mouth will only make it worse. This is what I was afraid of.

CHAPTER 3

CHARITY (BELLANY)

On the inside, I'm totally laughing. A rift has started between these two, and I'm the cause of it. I couldn't be happier. This is perfect, and it happened naturally, with no planning on my part— that is so rare. Usually I have to do a lot more scheming.

When I first found out that Roy had a girlfriend, I knew there would be some work for me to do. But lucky me, Roy is well on his way to being single once again.

Samantha pushes her chest out. I'm positive this is an effort to ward me off and simultaneously remind Roy that she's the one he should be looking at. Desperate girl. She's plain vanilla. Her boring, limp hair is shoulder length. I bet Roy wishes Samantha had long hair like mine. She doesn't style it or even try to look pretty. Her hair is dry like straw, and it's a dishwater blond. She should really get some highlights and layers, definitely some extensions.

"So where are you from?" Samantha asks me.

How sweet. She's trying to be nice and get to know me. I don't buy it. I know it's all for show. She wants Roy to think that she's not intimidated by me, that she's a nice, friendly girl, someone deserving of his trust. I can see right through her act, and I wonder if Roy realizes how fake and insecure his girlfriend is. She doesn't want to get to know me. She wants me gone—period. If Samantha could get away with it, she'd probably threaten me, tell me to stay away from her boyfriend, *or else*! But this girl can't do anything. She's no match for me. I think Roy knows this too. He almost seems embarrassed that Samantha is trying so hard.

"She moved here from Texas," Roy answers for me, and he's talking fast. He sounds nervous. He's probably not a good liar, generally speaking, otherwise he wouldn't be acting this way. I was right when I pegged him to be a desirable companion for me—someone I could manipulate.

Experience has taught me that attaching myself to a bad boy doesn't work, especially in situations like mine. I need a guy who's mostly good, with only an underlying layer of naughtiness; a boy who can be tipped over to his darker side with some nudging. The perfect guy for me can't already live in that space. He has to have a conscience—at least in the beginning.

I'm describing exactly who Quentin used to be, before I got him to do all that shameful stuff. Poor Quentin. Sometimes I still miss him, but not enough to be sad or lose any sleep—nothing like that. He's just a distant memory.

"Texas?" Samantha asks. "You just don't sound like you're from Texas."

"Oh really? How are people from Texas supposed to sound? Do they talk like this?" I say with a slow, exaggerated drawl. "Or maybe you recognize them from their giant belt buckles and Stetsons."

"Well, no, I just thought that…" She shakes her head. "Never mind."

That's what I thought. You're no match for me.

I always like winning an argument, but the exchange makes me think. I need to be careful. I grew up in North Carolina, so I can produce a pretty convincing Southern accent when I want to. But I really shouldn't use it. It could give me away. I don't want anyone to recognize me for who I really am, a fugitive on the run.

CHAPTER 4

SAMANTHA

I'm so jealous I could cry.

Roy never had a girlfriend before me, but lots of girls have liked him. My friend Tracy is the one who set us up on a double date. She kept encouraging Roy to ask me out, until he finally did.

If it hadn't been for Tracy's meddling, I don't think we would be together. That's the part of our history that I hate. I wish he would have been the one to pursue me, instead of Tracy pushing him to do it. Sometimes I wonder if Roy even likes me in a romantic way. Does he think about me when I'm gone? Does he miss me?

Twice last week, I asked him if he wanted me to come over after I was done working on the yearbook. It was going to be slightly late, but not that late.

He barely even thought about it. His response was so quick: "No, don't worry about it. I'll see you tomorrow morning at school."

The second time I asked him, he dismissed me even quicker. Now I'm connecting the dots. His lack of time for me leads straight to Charity.

The longer I look at her, the more hopeless I feel. My chest continues to constrict as I stare at her tiny waist. And those long legs are sure to grab the attention of any boy who has a heartbeat. What size is she? A two? A one? Is there a size one?

I used to think that I wouldn't have to worry about another girl drawing his attention. The girls around here are all too trashy for Roy's taste. But I've got a suspicion that Charity is a trashy girl in disguise. I just wish Roy could see it somehow.

Charity is smiling again. Did I miss something? I hate when my mind wanders off. I smile back. If nothing else, at least Roy will know I'm being friendly.

"Achoo."

She just sneezed and it sounded like a tiny mouse. Seriously? Could she be any more dainty and cute?

"Bless you," Roy says with a chuckle. Great. He does think she's cute. I know he does.

"Allergies?" I ask her, hoping she has at least one flaw.

She waves her hand in front of her nose like she's trying not to sneeze again. But the urge passes and she blushes.

Roy chuckles again. And I'm clenching my teeth.

"Don't laugh at me," Charity says as if she's embarrassed. Get real. I bet that sneeze was fake. No way is she embarrassed. Miss Perfect probably never gets embarrassed.

Roy covers his mouth to stifle another laugh. "Sorry. But that was probably the tiniest sneeze I have ever heard."

"I hate my sneeze," she says, all shy-like. "I think it's just the dust from changing the light bulb."

"I told you I would do it for you. You didn't have to do it."

She's smiling again. Oh stop. Just stop! I need him to get away from her. "Roy, do you want to go work on that homework assignment that's due tomorrow?" I ask, pointing over my shoulder at his grandmother's house.

He looks at me and blinks as if he's confused.

"For marketing class?" I prompt him. We're in the same class. He knows the assignment is due tomorrow.

"Yeah, marketing." He places his hand on my shoulder, looking me in the eye. I love it when he looks at me all intense-like. It's as if there's nobody else in the world more important to him than me. "Let me go get my backpack out of the office."

"Me too. I left mine in my car. I'll meet you back here." Partway through the parking lot I stop, turn back around, and see Charity with milk crates in hand following Roy into the hotel.

I quickly snap a picture of her and send it to Tracy, then type out a text: Roy's next girlfriend. Tracy is gonna flip when she sees this. She'll try to make me feel better by telling me that Roy will never dump me—that he loves me. But Roy has never told me that he loves me. Our relationship isn't that intense or serious. I wish it was, but now I don't think it will ever be like that. If anything, our relationship is on the brink of destruction.

A loud engine rumbles nearby. It's coming from a blue pickup truck that has just pulled into a parking space. The guy sitting behind the wheel nods and smiles at me as I walk past him. So many strangers come and go here all the time. I'm still not quite used to it. When I glance back over my shoulder at him, I see that he's holding his phone up in front of his face. Is he taking a picture of me? No, that can't be what he's doing. He's probably just reading something like an email or a text message.

CHAPTER 5

ROY

Samantha is sitting across the table from me. I look up from my laptop several times and catch her staring. Each time she looks away and continues doing her homework. Normally she is more focused than this.

"Is something wrong?" I finally ask.

"No," she replies without hesitation.

I catch her looking at me again, only this time I smile. I expect her to smile back but she seems lost in thought. I close my laptop, reach across the table and take her hand in mine. "Ready for a break?"

She nods, studying my face as if she's trying to see something in my expression that's not there. I'm pretty sure she wants to know if I'm cheating on her. But I'm not. "Come on, let's go see if my grandma's still got some of that chocolate cake in the fridge that I told you about." Samantha loves chocolate.

I eat two huge slices and she only eats half of one. She's mostly picking at it with her fork. Usually Samantha devours Grandma's cakes. Then I realize I didn't get us anything to drink. I quickly swipe a gallon of milk from the fridge. "Sorry," I say, still chewing on a mouthful. I swallow as I open the cupboard and grab two glasses. "I bet you're thirsty."

"Actually," Samantha wrinkles up her nose, "I think I'll just have water."

I look down at the two full glasses of milk. I guess I'll be drinking both of these. I push them aside and pour her a glass of water.

Normally she'll drink milk or a diet soda of some kind. She usually doesn't ask for water. Maybe she's really thirsty today.

She takes the glass in her hand and doesn't drink it.

"Do you…want some ice?" I ask, wondering if that's the problem.

She shakes her head. "No. This is fine." She takes the tiniest sip.

I down both of the glasses of milk. Grandma hates it when food goes to waste, and I guess I've adopted her philosophy.

Samantha pushes her plate toward me. "I'm full."

I pick up her fork and start eating the rest of her cake. "More for me." Once again I give her a smile and she doesn't smile back.

I wish she would. Samantha has a smile that covers her whole face. Her nose scrunches, and her eyes light up. She can tend to be serious and overly focused at times. But when I catch her in the right mood it's fun to get her laughing.

It's a lot easier with Charity. I don't have to work for it at all. She smiles a lot, all on her own. Each time I talk to her, she finds something to joke and laugh about.

This one time, she had me come look at a room that some guy had thoroughly trashed. "You've gotta see this. It's a masterpiece of filth," she said.

She wasn't exaggerating. The guy stayed for over a week without any visits from housekeeping.

"He said he didn't want to be disturbed. Look at this and tell me the person responsible is not disturbed," she laughed.

Charity had me haul away six huge garbage bags packed full of trash that she collected from his room. It couldn't have been a pleasant experience to have to clean up after him. I thought she might quit, but instead she found reasons to joke about it.

Samantha stares at me with that same unreadable look on her face again. I feel guilty that I've let my thoughts wander to Charity. Can she tell?

I rinse and stack our plates, wondering what she's thinking.

"I don't want to do homework anymore," Samantha says, breaking the silence.

"Okay, what do you want to do?" I ask.

"Come here." She moves to the couch and pats the spot next to her. "How about we sit for a while?" She has that same tone in her voice that she always gets when she wants to kiss me, or wants me to kiss her. I'm kind of surprised, though. She's been acting distant. I glance at the clock, and Samantha notices.

"Oh, your grandma is coming home soon, isn't she."

I nod. "Probably any minute."

"Well, we better hurry then." She pats the couch again.

I move quickly to sit, grab hold of her hand, and look into her beautiful eyes. The one on the right is green, mixed with brown. The one on the left is pure golden caramel. Nobody else has eyes like hers. She thinks they're weird. I don't. I told her before that she's one of a kind.

My gaze travels down her face, past the light sprinkling of freckles across the bridge of her nose and cheeks. She hates her freckles, but I like them. My fingers squeeze tighter around her hand as I lean in. Her lips are soft as always, the fit against mine a perfect match. I want to show her by the way I kiss her that she shouldn't worry about losing me.

A series of beeps fill the air. It's the combination lock on the door. We both pull away. The door is starting to open. I look back at Samantha. We kiss again. It's quick, but it's even more intense than before.

"I'm here," Grandma announces loudly. Roscoe barks as he races over to see her. Old guy. He must have been asleep in her bedroom.

After he gets scratches and love from Grandma, he races over to see me. I pull him onto the couch. Samantha smiles as she pets him. "He's such a cute dog." I'm so glad she's happy now.

"Hello, Roscoe. Have you been a good boy today?" Samantha talks to him like he's a baby, and he loves it. He jumps into her lap, his tiny tail wagging.

"Hi, Mrs. Crawly," Samantha says. "Can I help you with anything?"

Grandma doesn't answer her. She peers over at me. "What do you feel like eating tonight? Steak? Fish?"

For some reason Grandma has never warmed up to Samantha. I place a hand on her knee. "What do you feel like eating?"

Samantha claps her hands together. "Steak sounds good." I guess she's hungry now; another good sign.

I nod in agreement. "Yeah. Steak sounds good."

"Steak it is."

Samantha starts talking to Roscoe again. Whatever was bothering her before, I guess she's over it now.

CHAPTER 6

SAMANTHA

I set the table, wondering if the fork goes on the right and the knife on the left. I have no idea but even if it is right, I'm sure Veronica will have a problem with it. All I ever do is try to be nice to that lady so she'll like me, but it feels like an impossible quest sometimes. Whenever I help out, she tells me I'm "doing it wrong." The mail is put away in the *wrong* pile. The dishes are stacked the *wrong* way. The towels are folded *wrong*—never mind the fact that I fold them the same way she does.

Sometimes I wonder if Veronica thinks I'm not good enough for Roy, that I'm the *wrong* girl. Sometimes I wonder about that myself too. Am I good enough for him?

My best friend, Tracy, gave me some good advice once. She said, *Just be your true self. Stop trying so hard.* I wish I could remember to do that.

Surprisingly Veronica doesn't criticize my table-setting skills, but as soon as I cut into my steak, I see there's a new problem. It's way too bloody. I told Veronica that I wanted my steak well done. I think Roy noticed that I'm not eating it. He keeps looking at my plate. He's probably worried I'll offend Veronica if I don't eat every last bite. But I just can't make myself do it.

The rareness of my steak isn't the only thing that's bothering me. I'm still worried about Roy and Charity. I have zero trust that she'll leave him alone. I think she's going to pursue him hard, and I suspect she has already been doing this. What's more, I'm afraid either Roy knows this is happening and likes it, or he is naive and will let it happen just the same.

"Pass the salt," Veronica says.

I hand the saltshaker to her, wondering if it would be awkward for me to bring up Charity. There's so much I don't know about her, so much I'm curious about. I'm sure there's a long story behind her arrival here.

I smile at Veronica. She doesn't smile back, but that's normal. "So I met Charity for the first time today. She seems nice," I say.

"Oh yes. Isn't she a lovely girl?"

"How did you meet her?"

"Through Jesse. He told me she was low on money, and needed a place to stay. He begged me to hire her and set her up in a hotel room, telling me what a hard worker she is and how much his customers like her. I thought I was doing him a favor, but it wound up being the other way around. Charity has been a great addition."

Veronica stabs a piece of steak with her fork, swirling it in the blood on her plate. As if her looks aren't enough, everyone thinks Charity is a saint. Jesse likes her. Veronica likes her. How can Roy not fall for her? I might be the only person who has a bad vibe about her. But if something is too good to be true, then it must not be true. She must have some flaws. I wonder why Charity suddenly showed up in Chehalis without any money or a place to live. "How did Jesse meet her?"

"Just by chance. She showed up one day asking for a job, said she was trying to lay low for a while."

Lay low? I don't like the sound of that. People who have nothing to hide don't need to lay low. I glance over at Roy, who doesn't seem bothered at all to hear this. I guess he must already know the story behind the mysterious Charity. "Why does Charity need to lay low?"

Veronica's mouth is full of food, so Roy answers, "She's trying to hide from her ex-boyfriend."

Immediately my mind starts swirling with more questions. Did her ex try to kill her or threaten her? Was he abusive? Or did she do something to make him want to get even with her? Did she steal from him? Did she burn his house down? What's the story?

I reach for another roll and set it on my plate, then start smearing butter onto it. "That sounds serious. Did she say why she has to hide from him?"

Veronica lowers her glass of milk, setting it down on the table. "It is serious. Her ex has already tried to kidnap her once before. She barely managed to get away. There was no time to go back to her apartment and pack up any of her things. She had to leave with the clothes on her back, no purse, no ID, no money. Luckily someone at the bus station took pity on her and bought her a bus ticket. That's how she ended up here."

I'm not so sure I believe this story, but Roy seems perfectly accepting of every word coming out of Veronica's mouth. The whole thing seems too convenient: no ID, no money, no clothes, nowhere to go. I think she's hiding something. I'm surprised Veronica doesn't think so too.

I'm kind of nervous about questioning Veronica any further about Charity's situation, but I feel like I have to. Charity is a stranger. Who knows what kinds of things she has done in the past, or what kinds of things she's capable of doing in the future? "Wow, that's a lot to go through." I tear apart my roll and continue, "But I wonder… No one in Chehalis had ever heard of Charity until recently, right? How do we know she's telling the truth?"

"You think she's lying?" Roy asks.

"Well, people don't always tell the truth. It's just a fact of life."

Roy arches an eyebrow. "Until she gives me a legitimate reason not to believe her, I'm going to give her the benefit of the doubt. I think we all should."

I'm not happy at all to hear him defend her. Why did he feel like he needed to do that?

Veronica asks me to pass the pepper. She shakes it over her mashed potatoes. "Hopefully Charity will be able to save up some money soon and get a place of her own."

I don't think things are going to be quite that simple. "I hope so. But what if her ex comes looking for her and he finds her here at the hotel? According to her, this guy is dangerous. Do you think it's safe to expose yourselves and your hotel guests to this kind of volatile situation?"

Roy is looking at me with a strange expression on his face. I think my logic is sound, and I don't regret expressing my concern. Does he have a problem with it?

"She doesn't have anywhere else to go, Samantha," he says.

Veronica lets out a loud, "Ha!"

I shoot her a confused look.

"Dangerous?" she says, then adds another, "Ha!" Veronica genuinely seems amused. I don't think this is funny. "Samantha, my dear, I'd bet at least half the people who stay at the hotel are capable of stirring up trouble and could be classified as dangerous." She makes air quotes with her fingers when she says the word *dangerous*. "I'm sure we've had murderers, rapists, kidnappers, all kinds of criminals stay here. If I wanted to avoid all the bad people in the world, I wouldn't be running a hotel."

Okay, now I feel like an idiot. I guess I never thought of the hotel business that way. I'm embarrassed I brought it up. I scoop some more mashed potatoes onto my plate and then some carrots.

Veronica looks at my plate, specifically at my steak. "Are you not hungry?" she asks.

Didn't she just see me get a second helping of mashed potatoes and carrots? Doesn't that count for something? "Yeah, I'm hungry," I say, then take another bite of potatoes.

Veronica picks up her knife to cut into her steak again, and I see her give Roy a look when she thinks I'm not paying attention.

I grab another roll and start buttering it. "Doesn't Charity have any family?"

Roy looks at Veronica. I suspect he doesn't know the answer to this question.

"Charity said she grew up in foster care and doesn't know what happened to her biological parents. It's a real tragic story. She was left at a fire station as an infant. She got adopted once, but the couple who adopted her died in a fire—real sad situation. So she went back into foster care and never got adopted again."

How convenient. She doesn't have any parents, no siblings, no grandparents, nobody. What a bunch of garbage. "How old is she?" I ask.

Veronica pauses to think again. "Eighteen. She said she took her GED instead of finishing out her senior year."

How convenient, again. She's the same age as Roy and a damsel in distress, waiting for her prince charming to come save her. She probably has a loose glass slipper somewhere for him to find.

Roy picks up his plate and takes it into the kitchen without asking me if I'm through eating. He usually never leaves the table without me. This isn't good.

"Listen, hun," Veronica says. "How about we cool it with all this talk about Charity? I've already said way too much. And I don't like to gossip."

That's a lie. Veronica loves to gossip. She does it all the time. She spreads all kinds of rumors about her hotel guests, especially if she thinks one of them is cheating on a spouse. She blabs that kind of stuff all around town.

I take my plate into the kitchen and follow Roy to the living room, wondering if he's mad at me too.

CHAPTER 7

ROY

Samantha is being quiet again. Maybe she's mad. I defended Charity, but I felt like I had to. Samantha seems determined to find something wrong with her, and if she can't find anything she's going to make something up. If she'd just give Charity a chance, she'd see how grateful Charity is for this opportunity. She puts forth the work and effort required to pay for her room. She always says "thank you," and she's friendly to the hotel guests. I don't think there's a single thing wrong with her. She's had a hard life, and she's finally caught a break.

Roscoe is whining at my feet, so I pick him up and set him on my lap. "Do you want to pet him?" I ask Samantha and she shakes her head no. Okay, I'm getting tired of this. "What's wrong?"

"Nothing."

"Samantha, I know something's wrong. Will you please talk to me?" I really do want to talk to her, and I really do want to hear what's bothering her.

"I don't really feel like talking about it."

"Why is that?"

"Because you're not going to listen to me. You never listen to me."

Sometimes she can be so infuriating and stubborn. Roscoe rolls over onto his back so I can pet his belly, which is quite a contrast to what Samantha is doing right now. She's sitting here with her arms folded tightly across her chest, glaring at the TV like she wants to murder it.

I can hear Grandma's slippered feet sliding across the floor as she enters the living room. "You two kids gonna just sit on your butts while I do all the dishes?"

"Sorry, Grandma. I'll take care of it."

"My arthritis is acting up. I'm heading to bed. Come on, Roscoe. Let's go."

Samantha follows me into the kitchen, and we manage to clean everything without saying a single word to each other. The air around us is thick with tension, and I just want to be able to breathe again. There's gotta be something I can do or say to lighten the mood and snap her out of this.

I'm about to pull the plug to drain the water out of the sink, but I stop. I had put way too much soap in the water, and it's still full of soapsuds. I scoop up a handful of soapsuds and stick it on my chin, making myself a white, frothy beard. "How about a kiss?" I wiggle my eyebrows at Samantha. There's no way she's going to be able to keep a straight face, not when I look like this.

Samantha backs away a step, a smile emerging on her face. "Get away from me."

I scoop up another handful and stick it to my cheeks, making a full beard. Then I extend my arms out in front of me like I'm a zombie and slowly start walking toward her. "Kiss me, Sammy. Give me a big wet one."

Samantha bursts into a full smile and tosses a wet rag at me, but my reflexes are too quick. She misses and takes off running. "Get away from me, you weirdo!"

"Kiss me, Sammy! Please! Kiss me!"

She's squealing and laughing as she tears through the house. We're running around the kitchen table, and her feet slip out from under her. I catch her just in time, wrapping my arms around her. She tries to resist me at first, but my lips find hers, and I know she wanted this—I can tell by her reaction.

Lucky for her, most of the soapsuds have already fallen off my face. I doubt there's much left to transfer onto her as we kiss. But that wasn't the point of all of this. I wanted her to be happy again. I wanted her to forgive me. And, I wanted to feel her soft lips against mine one more time.

There's a knock at the door.

"Are you expecting anybody?" Samantha asks.

My mind is a bit of a blur right now, so I don't stop to think about her question. I just answer the door to get rid of whoever this is.

Samantha follows me, holding my hand. As soon as the door opens, her fingers let go of mine. Charity is standing on the porch, and my instinct is that I should shut the door right in her face—not that I really would, I just wish I hadn't opened the door at all.

"What are you doing here?" Samantha says at my side.

I'm shocked she said that out loud. Usually she isn't so rude. This is definitely new behavior, and I don't like it.

Charity raises her eyebrows, seemingly at a loss for words. I feel caught in the middle, not sure what to say. Samantha's behavior was uncalled for. Charity didn't know she was interrupting. Man, I really wish I hadn't opened the door.

"I'm sorry. Am I interrupting something?" Charity asks.

Yeah. She knows she is. I don't think this could be any more awkward. I bet she wishes she would have never come here tonight. "Ah, it's fine," I reply, and I wipe my hand across my face just in case there's still soapsuds on it.

She smiles, hesitating. "I was wondering if you and Veronica are planning to play poker again tonight."

I should have known Charity would come over to play poker. Grandma gave her an open invitation. Samantha knows all about poker night, but she hasn't come over to play since she joined the yearbook committee. Sometimes Mack, the guy who runs Grandma's campground, or Jesse, the owner of the diner, joins us too. We don't gamble with real money, just poker chips and M&M's. Grandma usually has some kind of dessert to share, like the chocolate cake Samantha and I finished off earlier.

Samantha lets out a heavy sigh, full of irritation. "Veronica is already in bed."

Charity nods and the smile falls from her face. "Oh, okay. Yeah, I guess it's kinda late."

It's really not that late. Charity is just trying to be polite, unlike Samantha. Somehow, I've got to clear the air between these two. This awkwardness, this animosity, it needs to stop. I'm sure Samantha would feel a lot more comfortable with Charity if she could just get to know her and realize what a nice person she is, so I decide to ask Samantha, "Do you want to play poker?"

Samantha stands there, not speaking, not answering my question. She's just staring at me. I'm wondering if I should ask her again, except I know she heard me. Finally, she takes a deep breath, and I half-expect her to yell at me, but she exhales instead.

"I don't feel like playing poker tonight," she says in a sharp tone.

Charity takes a step back, and smiling says, "That's okay. Good night." As she turns to head down the porch steps, Samantha slams the door shut, really hard. The pictures on the wall shake.

"That was rude," I say. I'm not yelling or raising my voice. I'm merely making a statement of fact.

Samantha's mouth drops open. "I'm rude?" She points at the door. "Before Charity got here, we were having a good time, enjoying a private moment, and then you ruined everything by inviting her to stay. I haven't been over here to hang out with you in weeks. Sometimes I wonder if you even care about me."

Where did that come from? How could she think that I don't care about her? "Of course I care about you."

"Oh really? So when were you going to tell me about Charity living at the hotel, or your late-night poker games with her?"

She made that sound really bad, but it's not; it's nothing like that. I've been trying really hard not to let myself develop feelings for Charity, and to keep my distance. It's been hard. I deserve some credit. "All we've done is play poker and eat junk food. You know how it is." I really wish Samantha would just stop being mad at me. All I want to do is make her happy.

"Well, being that I'm your girlfriend, I would prefer it if you didn't play poker with Charity anymore."

This is an impossible request. She's got to know that. I take Samantha's hand in mine, hoping she'll calm down. "This isn't my house," I say calmly. "If my grandma wants to play poker, she's going to invite over whomever she wants to play with."

Samantha looks at me wide-eyed. This isn't the reaction I hoped for.

"You should come and play, like you used to. I'd rather have you here than Charity. You're way more fun than she is." Whew, there. I think I saved it.

Samantha pulls her hand away, folding her arms. "Why am I more fun, because I lose all the time?"

I wait a beat before I answer her. "Yes," I say with a straight face.

She socks me in the shoulder, not hard, and a slight smile escapes her lips, which I think she doesn't want me to notice. "I'm a good player. The only reason why you win is because you cheat." She pokes me in the chest.

"I don't cheat," I chuckle. "You're the one who cheats."

She pokes me in the chest again, and I grab hold of her wrist, pulling her in. I wrap my arms around her. She doesn't resist or fight. She melts into me. I think everything's going to be okay, at least for now.

CHAPTER 8

ROY

S itting at the front desk of the hotel with my homework spread out in front of me, I can't focus. My mind keeps running over my conversation with Samantha today at school. Seeing her is usually the most enjoyable part of the day, but she had to bring up Charity and her scary ex-boyfriend again.

"I wonder what he looks like?" she'd asked. As if I'd know.

"Why does it matter?" I asked. It seemed like a strange question to me.

"Well…" Samantha hesitated before saying more, which made me rethink my initial assumption. Maybe she didn't want to argue about Charity. Maybe there was a good reason, or maybe something had happened. Possibilities raced through my mind.

Samantha seemed to pick up on how concerned I was. "Oh, nothing bad happened," she said. "It's just, there was this loud pickup in the parking lot at the hotel yesterday when I went to grab my backpack. I thought a guy inside tried to take my picture."

She explained that she saw him again this morning in the parking lot of Jesse's Diner where Charity also works. It surprised me to find out that Samantha was actually concerned about Charity. I thought she was jealous of her.

"Thank you for telling me," I said, and I assured her that I would be on the lookout. But the description Samantha gave me was not helpful at all. He might have had a beard, or maybe just a mustache. He might have been tall, but he was sitting down so she really didn't know. He may have been young, but his face was kind of in a shadow.

And as for the pickup truck, she didn't know if it was a Ford, a Chevy, she had no idea what make and model it was. She shrugged and said, "I don't know. It was just a normal pickup truck."

Rearranging my homework in hopes it will keep my attention, I wonder if I should mention anything to Charity about this guy. I don't want to alarm her over something that might be nothing, nor do I want her to think that I'm some paranoid guy who has nothing better to do than to scrutinize every new person who shows up in town. I'm sure Charity's already under enough stress as it is, and I don't feel like I should be piling on.

My phone buzzes with a text from Samantha: I'm not going to be able to come over today. I've got too much homework and my dad said he wants to take me out to dinner tonight.

Her dad isn't a very attentive father, so this is good news. I'm sure she's excited to spend some time with him. I type out a reply: Enjoy dinner! Make him take you someplace nice.

She replies: Not McDonald's?

I laugh out loud. Her dad used to frequent that place, especially when she was younger. Samantha had a huge collection of Happy Meal toys.

I was thinking Chuck E. Cheese, I text back, remembering how upset she was when her dad took her there for her eighteenth birthday.

My phone buzzes with her response: He knows better than that! Haha!

I'm about to text her back when the hotel phone rings. The caller ID says it's Grandma. She's calling from the house. "Hi, Grandma."

"Roy. My arthritis is acting up. You're going to have to keep an eye on things for me. There's only one reservation tonight, and they might be coming in late."

"Got it. I'll stay here until they arrive. Do you need me to do anything for you?"

"No, I'll be all right. I've got Roscoe here to keep me company."

Good old Roscoe. "Call if you need me."

"I'm not helpless. I'm just old."

"I know, Grandma."

When I hang up the phone, I look around at the empty hotel lobby and settle on the mounted moose head. It came from Grandpa. He brought it back from a hunting trip in Alaska. He said that the moose tried to kill him and almost succeeded because his gun jammed.

A painting of a bald eagle hangs above the big stone fireplace. It was the last painting Mom completed before she died. Mom did a lot of paintings, and Grandma's entire house is filled with them. Her favorite subject to paint was the bald eagle. But she did other wildlife too: bears, deer, moose. She traveled around exhibiting her paintings, and she used to have her own art studio in town.

I don't often allow myself to look at that particular painting hanging above the fireplace, because it sometimes makes me feel depressed. Grandma said it has the opposite effect on her. It's weird how people handle grief differently. Maybe one day it will get easier for me to look at Mom's work and appreciate it.

Since I'm still stuck here waiting for the hotel guest to show up, I order pizza for dinner, and force myself to start on my homework. I don't want my GPA to drop with graduation only a few months away. Once my pizza arrives I start playing a game online with some of my friends from school. I usually do this when I cover the front desk. Grandma always keeps me busy with different responsibilities at the hotel, not all of them quite as chill as this.

It was her idea to build a hotel that had fireplaces in the more expensive rooms. I don't know if it brings in a lot of extra money, but it's a lot of work for me. I'm the one who shovels out the ashes, cleans the fireplaces, cuts down the trees, and chops the wood. The good part is, the work got me ripped.

The high school basketball coach noticed and wanted me to try out for the team. I enjoy playing, but Grandma needs my help around here—especially since Grandpa died. I don't have time for basketball.

This hotel is my life, and Samantha has been really patient and understanding about my responsibilities here. She doesn't seem to mind when our Friday and Saturday nights are spent sitting behind the counter, waiting for guests to arrive.

When the hotel lobby door swings open, I'm hopeful for a second, thinking it's going to be the late-arriving guest. But it's Charity. She's wearing her waitress uniform, so she probably just got off work. She looks tired.

"Want some pizza?" I ask her. "It's pepperoni."

Her face lights up. "Yes! I'm starving."

She eats four slices and downs two cans of Coke, which surprises me because she's so skinny.

"What game are you playing?" She motions to the computer.

I give her a brief rundown of the game, and she seems really into it, which is shocking. Samantha hates this kind of stuff. I offer to set her up on Grandma's computer so we can play together, and she actually says yes.

"This is going to be fun," I say as I log in to the computer and pull up the game for her. "Trust me, you're gonna love it." I think Samantha would love it too if she would just give it a chance.

Charity takes off her jacket and pulls her long hair back into a ponytail. Something about seeing her neck exposed like that draws me in. Maybe it's her flawless bronze skin, or the angle of her jawline, or the—what am I doing? My eyes clamp shut for a couple beats. I've got to stop this. I'm not a freakin' vampire on the lookout for a neck to sink my fangs into. I gotta get ahold of myself.

Charity places her hand on the mouse and wiggles it around,

positioning the cursor at the right spot on the screen. "I'm not very good at this stuff, but I'll give it my best shot."

"Sounds good to me."

I explain to her how to play, wondering if I'll have to repeat myself multiple times and answer a bunch of questions. I had to do that with Samantha, when I tried to teach her. Thankfully, it's much easier with Charity. Once I explain things, she quickly comprehends and waits for the next bit of instruction. It's like her brain is a sponge. She is locked in, totally absorbed. She must be naturally wired for gaming. I bet I could play something more challenging with her and she'd probably really get into it.

I take a seat at the counter, glad she's sitting behind me so that I'm not tempted to stare at her. The only thing more distracting than a hot girl is a hot gaming girl. I put my headphones on and look back over my shoulder to make sure she's all set, even though I already know she is. I'm just trying to be polite.

Charity smiles and gives me a thumbs-up. I really hope she likes this game, because I wouldn't mind making this more of a regular thing. If Samantha saw that Charity was into this, maybe she'd finally decide to give it a try. Samantha wasn't interested in playing poker at first either, but after she tried it, she was hooked.

CHAPTER 9

CHARITY (BELLANY)

Jackpot. I'm logged on to Veronica's computer, thanks to Roy. Sometimes he's way too naive. He's just a small-town boy who has no idea who or what he's dealing with. I am going to corrupt him and turn his life upside down. It's gonna be an adrenaline rush.

I crack my knuckles and begin typing away on the keyboard. *Let's see what kind of good stuff is on here… Oh look. Veronica's browser history hasn't been cleared; time to follow the money.* I click the link to a bank account, and a huge smile spreads across my face. This is too easy. All of her information automatically fills in. I peek over the monitor and see the back of Roy's head, then grab my phone and discreetly snap a picture of my screen with Veronica's username and password displayed.

As I look over her banking transactions, I discover that she has written a ton of checks. Who writes checks anymore? I click on one of the images to enlarge it: two hundred dollars to a Todd Sims. I actually know this guy. He and his wife come to eat at the diner all the time. He's a horrible tipper and always wants to sit in my section. His wife is nice, but he seems odd. I wonder what this money is for. I scroll down and discover that Veronica has paid him the same amount every month like clockwork. It has been going on for a while.

I click on another check image. This one is made out to Joshua Iverson in the amount of five hundred dollars. I don't know him. I don't think he comes to the diner, unless he sits in Sloan's section.

Roy turns around and takes off his headphones. I hover the cursor over the X in case I need to close everything. *Stay right where you are, Roy*, I think to myself.

"Are you getting bored yet?" he asks.

Judging by the look on his face, he hopes I'll say no. Well, he's in luck. "I'm having fun. Let's keep playing."

"Okay, let me know if you want to do something else."

I nod and then he spins back around in his chair. That was easy enough. I toggle into the game and do enough to make my presence felt, then switch back to the real action.

I continue sifting through Veronica's browser history and discover that she has four different bank accounts. Why does she need so many? Maybe one is for the campground. She might have even more businesses I don't know about yet. She recently mentioned that she sold her rental houses, and I find the bank account that she dumped all that money into. The last time she logged in to this account was six weeks ago.

There's another account that she hasn't accessed in eight months. When I see how much money is in here, I feel like my eyes are going to pop out of my head. There's over three million dollars. Bingo. This is the account I'm going to siphon money out of. For starters, I'll purchase ten grand through a cryptocurrency exchange. I'll use a tumbler to anonymize it and then cash it out through a peer-to-peer service.

Roy turns around again and pulls his headphones off. "Let's play for another five minutes, How does that sound?"

"Sounds good." I guess he noticed that my player isn't doing much. I've kind of just left it sitting idle.

As I close all of the open windows on my screen, I imagine what I'll spend that first ten thousand dollars on. I need to buy some new clothes and some shoes, plus makeup. Not to mention, I definitely need to get my hair done and get a manicure.

I lift up a stack of papers on Veronica's desk and find her checkbook. This is just way too easy. It's like everything is literally being handed to me tonight. I'm tempted to rip out a couple blank checks and stuff them into my pocket. I doubt she'll even notice they're missing. I almost put the checkbook back, but then I stop. Roy's headphones are still on. He won't be able to hear me rip these checks out. I quickly snatch a couple and slide them into my pocket.

Most of the time when I smile it's fake, not because I'm happy. But right now, I'm ecstatic. It is so hard to stop myself from smiling from ear to ear as I sit here. Dollar signs keep rolling around in my head. *I could kiss you, Roy. You have absolutely made my night.*

Actually, maybe I will kiss you.

CHAPTER 10

ROY

Charity is one of the worst players I've ever played against in this game. It looks like computer games aren't her thing after all. But she's still smiling, so maybe she enjoyed it. I'm about to ask her if she wants to play a game of chess, which is kind of nerdy, but it's something I like to do. Plus I get the sense that she'll probably be good at it. She seems really smart.

We are interrupted just then by the late-arriving hotel guest. While I get him checked in, Charity tidies up the lobby and takes care of our trash from the pizza. I log off the computers, lock up the cash drawer, and slip the keys into my pocket.

I'm following Charity through the lobby, expecting to shut the lights off and lock the door behind us, when she turns and sits down on one of the couches.

"Do you mind if we talk for a while?" she asks.

Charity isn't smiling anymore, which is unusual. Something must be bothering her. My thoughts quickly shift to the conversation I had with Samantha earlier at school today about that guy in the blue pickup truck. Does this have anything to do with him? Or maybe she wants to vent about Grandma. Sometimes Grandma can be a bit demanding.

I sit down on the couch, giving her plenty of room; mainly because I don't want to cross that line of friendship. The farther away from her I am, the better.

Charity leans forward to take off her apron. She tosses it over the arm of the couch, then takes her ponytail out, letting her hair down. I avert my eyes once I realize I'm staring. I don't know what my problem is. Hair up, hair down, it doesn't matter—I am way too attracted to her.

"I just feel overwhelmed right now."

"You do? Why?" I know she's working two jobs to support herself. That can't be easy.

"It's about my ex." Her voice is low, like she's afraid someone might overhear, even though it's just the two of us on the couch.

I wait, giving her space.

"When we first started seeing each other, he seemed…you know, chill. Like, easygoing, thoughtful. He brought me flowers while I was at work. It was sweet—at first." Her fingers twist in her lap. "Then it became more frequent. Twice a week…then more…and suddenly he was just there all the time. Always showing up."

"What did your boss say?" I ask.

She shakes her head. "They didn't like it. It was a problem. I told him not to come by or I could lose my job, but that didn't stop him. At first it was excuses: 'I was in the neighborhood,' or 'Thought you might want coffee.' But it stopped feeling thoughtful and started feeling like full-on surveillance."

She finally looks up at me, eyes glassy. "He'd get weird if I didn't text back right away. He'd ask who I was talking to. Who I sat next to at lunch. If I wore something new, he'd want to know who I was trying to impress."

I glance around, instinctively checking our surroundings, even though I know we're alone.

She pulls in a shaky breath. "I kept telling myself it would get better—that he'd eventually back off. But he never did. I'd try to break up with him, and he'd just flip out on me. Or show up and beg me to take him back...promising he'd change. And I—"

Her voice breaks, and she quickly swipes at a tear sliding down her cheek.

I lean in. "You don't have to keep talking about...whatever his name is."

She shakes her head. "I never say his name anymore. Saying it makes it real. Makes him real."

She wipes another tear off her cheek. "But I still need to talk about it. I've been keeping this stuff bottled up inside for so long, I feel like I'm gonna burst if I don't talk about it." She lets out a nervous-sounding laugh. "I bet you didn't expect to hear about all of this tonight, did you?"

No, I didn't expect to hear any of it. But I don't mind. "Just to warn you, I've been told that I'm a terrible listener," I tease. "But I'm trying to be better."

"I think you're a great listener."

Not according to Samantha. "Just don't quiz me on any of the facts. I might fail."

"Don't worry, I won't." She smiles, then pauses to gather her thoughts before she continues. "At first we would fight once in a while, you know, just argue over stupid stuff. But then one day he showed up at my work, accusing me of cheating on him. After that he insisted on driving me to and from work. I would catch him going through my phone and my computer. He made me give him all my passwords. He became so controlling that he wouldn't let me do anything by myself. He wouldn't even let me go to the grocery store without him.

"One night I told my friend to cover for me at work. I slipped out the back and just started running. I didn't have anywhere to go, but I felt so desperate." Tears are streaming down her face, and I'm not sure what I should do here. Should I give her a hug? Should I tell her everything's going to be all right? Should I just be quiet and listen?

No girl has ever spilled her guts to me like this before. Samantha doesn't really open up that much. I guess I just know her life story because we grew up together. The phrase "a closed book" seems to fit Samantha. What exactly goes through her mind, most of the time I haven't got a clue.

Charity looks at me, hesitating. I stare back at her, still not sure what I should do.

"He pulled a gun on me," she says, and my shoulders suddenly tense. "The bullet whizzed right by my ear…" She motions with her hand and continues talking, but I'm having a hard time processing what she's saying. My heart is racing, and my chest feels tight. Don't go down this rabbit hole, I tell myself. Stop thinking about this. But the memories from my own trauma five years ago keep surfacing in my mind. Nobody knows what happened to us back then…just me and Grandma.

I turn my attention to the moose head hanging on the wall, focusing on every little detail, trying to distract myself. Charity is still talking, but I barely process anything she says.

Eventually, Charity shifts the topic of conversation away from heavy things and moves on to her new life here. I'm able to push my own disturbing memories back out of mind again. My heart rate slows and I take a deep breath.

I'm listening to her more intently now. She is definitely a survivor. But the hard part still isn't over. Her ex is out there somewhere. What kind of life must Charity be living, always having to look over her shoulder and worry that this guy is going to suddenly show up here one day?

She places her hand on mine, looking up at me with her deep green eyes, and suddenly I'm feeling uncomfortable. Why is she touching me like that? She knows I'm going out with Samantha. Her fingers brush across the back of my hand, then glide along my wrist. The touch of her skin against mine feels way too good. She leans in slightly, and I think I know what's going to happen next. I can't let her do this—she knows I can't. So why am I still sitting here, letting her touch me? I've got to stop this before something happens that I'll regret. I stand up, my heart thrumming in my chest. I can't believe how close I was to ruining everything I have with Samantha. I'm so weak and pathetic.

"Thanks for listening to me," Charity says. She stuffs her apron into her pocket, then starts putting on her coat. When she stands up, a smile crosses her face. She holds her phone out. "Hey, do you mind if I take a selfie with you? I just realized I don't have a picture of me and my new best friend."

I'm her best friend? Is that what she thinks of me? Just a couple seconds ago, I could've sworn she was going to kiss me.

She squishes up close against me, holding her phone out.

"Whoa, hold up." I don't want her to take this picture. I blurt out the first lame excuse that comes to mind. "I never know what to do in photos. I don't look good."

"What?" she laughs. "Of course you do. You're sexy hot." She grabs hold of my arm, and my stomach dips. Does she not realize what her touch does to me?

CHAPTER 11

CHARITY (BELLANY)

I'm lying on the bed in my hotel room, phone in hand, looking at the picture I took of Roy. He is capital H-O-T. When I create our first photo album, I think I'll put this one on the cover. I look good, still have a tan even with the overcast skies here, thanks to a bit of help from the local tanning salon. Roy's laughing in the picture, and so am I. People frequently compliment me on my smile. I think Roy's smile is just as special but in a different way. His smile is more innocent, kind of shy.

When I first tried to take a photo with him, he didn't cooperate. He kept making funny faces. It took seven tries before I got him to hold still and actually pose with a normal smile. I wasn't mad that he was being silly—just the opposite. I loved that he was being playful. He kept trying to take my phone from me, insisting that he could take a better picture than me. I would have let him take my phone, but I was enjoying wrestling with him way too much. If Samantha would have walked in on us while that was going on, she would have flipped out—her head would have spun right off her neck.

At one point we were so close to each other, I thought he was going to kiss me. Our faces were literally inches apart. We both paused right there, staring at each other. The look in his eyes was intense. I wasn't sure if he was going to lean in and make the first move—I know he wanted to. His gaze lowered to my lips. Another second longer, it would have happened, I'm sure of it.

As I lay here thinking about all of those lies I told him—how my ex almost shot and killed me, how he controlled and abused me—I feel like I successfully managed to pull on Roy's heart-strings a bit. I purposely didn't mention my ex-boyfriend's name, Quentin. And I never will.

In reality, Quentin wasn't controlling or possessive of me when we were together. He never acted abusive toward me, not at first. I was the one who controlled and manipulated him. I had to help him understand that nothing was more important than me—not a basketball career, not school, not his car, and definitely not his sorry excuse for a mother.

He didn't become an abusive monster until we were on the run from the police. He cracked under the pressure. It ruined him. He wasn't eating, wasn't sleeping. One day the stress became too much and he finally lost his temper; he went ballistic and pushed me to the ground. He knew that I had hit my head on the tile floor. There was a loud crack. I reached back and felt wetness on the back of my head, then saw the blood on my fingers.

Quentin didn't apologize or try to help me. Instead, he grabbed our cash off the table—all of it—and stuffed it into his pocket, then he started packing his bag. He was going to leave me in that run-down hotel in the middle of nowhere, hurt, without transportation, without money. I couldn't let him do that to me. I had to stop him before he did something stupid and got us both caught by the police. So I did what anybody in my situation would've done.

I took care of the problem. It was just like what had happened back in North Carolina at the train tracks. Only this time, I used a brick instead of a rock.

The irony is that when I swung the rock I was doing it to save Quentin from his attacker.

When I swung the brick I was doing it to save myself from Quentin. I hit him with such force that he didn't get back up.

The only reason I ever bring up my abusive ex to people is so they will feel sorry for me and not judge me for wanting to live a quiet, inconspicuous life. Escaping an abusive ex-boyfriend is definitely a scenario that garners sympathy from people. Everybody here has been more than helpful. Well, everybody except for Samantha. But I understand why she acts the way she does. I am prettier than her, and smarter, much more of a catch. I am going to steal her boyfriend away, and she won't be able to stop me. That's just how it goes in life. The pretty girl gets any guy she wants. The homely girl gets nothing.

I tap my phone, switching to the next picture. This one was taken the other day when Samantha was walking to her car. It's weird how some people can look way better in a photograph than they do in person. She's definitely one of those people. Roy must like her for her personality. Although to me she seems seriously dull.

I grab my laptop and pull up some of the other pictures I have of Samantha. I took these while she was in the parking lot at her school hanging out with some of her friends. Thanks to my creative editing skills, I made one of the pictures look like Samantha is kissing some boy with wild hair. I saw her flirting with him, so I suspect she already likes him. I attach the picture to an email and send it to Roy. He'll never know it's from me. The name I'm using for this email account is Concerned Friend.

A smile spreads across my face as I imagine Roy's shock and outrage when he sees this. Yes, Roy, your girlfriend is seeking comfort in the arms of another boy. Time to dump her and move on to me.

I open a new tab and pull up a podcast I've been listening to by some guy named Cam Whitmeyer. He's been reporting on me and has way too many followers, which kind of makes me nervous. He's supposed to be interviewing Constance Perry's brother for today's episode. I'm curious about what her brother will say. I suspect he'll make a lot of threats and express his grief and outrage—all the usual predictable stuff. I doubt anyone will know the killer is a subscriber to this podcast, but I am.

The other reason I'm listening to Cam's podcast is because he seems bound and determined to track me down. While I highly doubt that he'll find me, I figure I should keep up with his investigative reporting, just in case.

CHAPTER 12

SAMANTHA

I'm waiting in my car for Tracy and her brother, Spike. School got out about ten minutes ago, so they should be here soon. As I'm sitting here, my attention is drawn to a guy wearing a cowboy hat and boots. He's walking across the parking lot, heading toward the school's main entrance. I know he's not from around here, otherwise he wouldn't be dressed like that. If he's a new student, he should really consider changing his wardrobe, because he definitely won't fit in here.

I look at my phone to check the time. I have a picture of me and Roy displayed on the home screen. We were so happy when that was taken—not so today. At lunch he didn't talk much. And he usually says goodbye to me after school before he heads to the hotel, but he didn't today. I want to know what's going on with him. Why is he acting strange? Does it have anything to do with Charity?

My thoughts are interrupted when Spike opens my car door. He slides into the front passenger seat next to me and holds out his phone to show me a video of our school's principal, Dr. Jennings, falling in the hallway.

"Check it out," Spike chuckles with that contagious laugh of his. "Boom, right there."

His laugh continues to fill the air, and I'm laughing too. Dr. Jennings slipped on a bologna sandwich and landed right on top of another student, who in turn spilled her Gatorade all over him.

Spike looks at me, a devious smile spreading across his face. "That's what Dr. Jennings gets. It's called karma."

I'm about to laugh again, but I'm kind of caught off guard by a thought that enters my mind: When did Spike turn into a handsome prince? He glances at me again, laughing as another video of the infamous fall starts playing on his phone, this one in slow motion with sound effects.

Tracy sticks her head in the door, hovering over Spike.

He pauses the video. "I called shotgun."

She rolls her eyes and climbs into the back of my convertible Mustang, knocking Spike forward into the dash. "Geez, you can at least be more gentle. I am fragile, you know."

My Mustang is not a classic beauty, nor is it something I'm sentimental about. It's over ten years old and the roof leaks sometimes, not a good match for rainy Washington. It only has two doors and the back seat barely has any legroom. So yeah, the front passenger seat is always the coveted spot. Spike tries to beat Tracy to it all the time. I used to tell him no, but lately I've enjoyed sitting next to him, way more than Tracy. She tends to be a backseat driver, from the front seat. She's always saying, *Watch out. Slow down. You're following too close.*

Tracy snaps her seat belt and grunts as she tries to get comfortable. She's almost five nine. Spike is only a couple inches taller, or is he? Actually, I think he just hit a growth spurt or something. Along with his cute dimples and his unruly, begging-to-be-touched hair, which is where he got his nickname from, he has somehow morphed into a hot guy overnight. But he is too young. He's a sophomore, and I'm a senior.

I look down at the screen of my phone as it lights up with a new text message. The photo that appears is one of me and Roy. My eyes slide back over to Spike, and I look away abruptly. What am I doing? I need to stop staring at him. I'm with Roy—handsome, rugged, kind Roy.

If Roy and I end up getting married one day, we'll be financially set. Veronica is loaded, and he's the sole heir to her fortune. Oh gosh, what am I thinking? Why am I dwelling on money and not love? Isn't love all that matters?

I put the car in reverse and glance in the rearview mirror at Tracy. She's been filling my head with this "heir to Veronica's fortune" bit for years, and now here I am dwelling on the same things as if they were my own thoughts. Well, I mean, it is my own thought, but I didn't come up with it on my own. Tracy is influencing me, in the wrong way. I'm not looking for a sugar daddy. I'm not a gold digger.

Suddenly more of Tracy's words come floating through my mind again, as if on cue: *People say money can't buy happiness, but it can sure make up for a whole lot of crap life throws at you.*

I feel like my life has been plagued with lots of problems. These problems are like the crap that gets stuck to the bottom of a shoe, wedged in all those tiny crevices, almost impossible to clean. Then the crap keeps stinking even after it has been cleaned off, because it's been tracked into the car, the house, the classroom at school—all the embarrassing places.

My dad is the one who leaves all of these crap piles for me to step in. I really love him, truly do, but he has a gambling problem. He'll say he's away at work and be gone for days, when in reality he's at the casino.

Our route takes us past Conifer Park Heights and I think about the beautiful home my family used to have there when my dad's business was booming. My mom was happy. I was happy. Everything seemed to be going great. But then my dad made some bad investment choices, racked up credit card debt, and turned to gambling as a remedy for his financial problems. That only made things worse.

My mom caught him lying to her several times, until she completely lost trust in him and they separated. She never asked if I wanted to go live with her. She just informed me that she was leaving. We rarely speak anymore, except for an occasional text message on my birthday or at Christmas.

There have been times when my dad's gambling has paid off, and he's won huge jackpots. Life would cruise along without any problems, then—bam! Crap happens. He blows all his money again in the cycle of: win some, lose some, win a little, lose way more, lose, lose, lose.

We're currently living in a run-down house in a terrible neighborhood. It's drafty, and smells like cat pee from the previous owners. The only reason I have my own vehicle is because I saved up babysitting money to buy it and because Roy gave me half of the money as a present for my eighteenth birthday.

"Watch out for the mailbox," Tracy calls from the backseat.

"I know," I mutter, trying not to get irritated.

Tracy once said if I ever break up with Roy, she wants him next, because he's rich. She hates being poor too.

I pull into the driveway of Tracy and Spike's house. This place isn't much better than the house I live in. Their front yard is full of weeds, mowed down as if they were grass. The screen door has a huge rip in it. The blinds covering the windows have pieces missing here and there, like someone took a pair of scissors to them and tried to make a paper snowflake. The front porch light is just a single light bulb, not a decorative fixture.

Spike turns to me before he opens the door to get out. "You should come in. Harry misses you."

"No thanks. I don't like tiny dinosaurs."

"He's a harmless iguana. He can't hurt you."

"He's creepy."

Tracy bangs on the back of the seat. "Spike. Let me out of here. I'm feeling claustrophobic. I swear I'm about to have a panic attack."

Spike quickly hops out so his sister can escape the grasp of my Mustang. She peers back inside before shutting the door. "I'll be right back. I'm just gonna go change."

Spike walks around to my window. I roll it down and give him a questioning look.

His hands rest on the door as he leans forward to stare at me. "You should really come inside." His voice takes on a different tone as he speaks, like that one sentence is loaded with a much deeper meaning.

Spike is not afraid to flirt. I used to be desensitized to him but then he changed, for the better. Way better. His skin is free from blemishes. His teeth, I don't know, I think he must have whitened them because they look great, and his hair that used to stick up, it's grown out and falls and flips quite perfectly.

"I'm going to Jesse's Diner with Tracy; I'll be back later. I'm spending the night tonight." I tell him this so he won't ask to come along.

"You are?" Spike's face lights up. "Sweet."

Tracy pokes her head out of the front door. "Spike, did you throw my jeans into the washing machine? I told you I was going to wear those."

"No, I didn't touch your jeans." He turns to me, walking backward, flashing me a white smile. "I'll see you later."

I realize I'm smiling back at him way too much and quickly drop the smile from my face.

CHAPTER 13

SAMANTHA

When I walk into Jesse's Diner with Tracy at my side, I can't see Charity anywhere. I thought she would be working tonight.

"How many?" a waitress with the name badge Sloan asks.

"Uh, can you seat us in Charity's section?" I reply.

She makes a face. "How many?"

"Two," Tracy replies, holding up two fingers.

Sloan walks slowly over to a table and drops a couple menus onto it. "She'll be right with you," she mutters as she walks away.

I've been eagerly anticipating this trip to the diner all day, hoping I would catch Charity looking less than perfect and watch her mess up at her job, so that Tracy and I could laugh about it later. Petty, I know. But still, it's what I'm hoping for.

"Hey, Samantha," Charity calls, crossing the diner with a smile on her face. "It's good to see you again."

Is it?

Tracy stiffens, exhaling sharply. "So fake."

I think Charity hears her, but she doesn't react. "How's it going?"

"Fine," I reply with my own fake smile.

"What can I get you to drink?"

Tracy frowns. "Water."

"Yeah, water for me too."

"Coming right up." She smiles big again as she turns to leave. Her uniform has a lace apron that ties in the back, and her dress has an ugly floral pattern on it, yet somehow she manages to make the look work for her. I swear she must have had it professionally tailored and dry cleaned. The other waitress is wearing the exact same outfit, only hers looks like someone stepped all over it.

I open the menu and check the prices. Tracy doesn't have any money to spend. This is my treat, but we aren't really here for the food. We're here for Charity.

"I do not like her," Tracy whispers. "She's so fake."

"I know," I say, so Tracy will stop repeating herself. I heard her the first time she said it.

Charity returns with two glasses of water, gliding across the floor all graceful and poised. "Here you go," she says, setting them down on the table. "So have you decided what you'd like to order?" Her voice is too sickly sweet. It's getting on my nerves.

Tracy shoves the menu at her. "I'll have the waffles."

I still haven't decided. "Are the waffles any good?" I ask, curious to learn if she'll give me an honest answer.

"The waffles here aren't anything special," Charity says, her voice low. "The cook just uses a basic mix and then adds water."

It doesn't escape my attention that Charity hadn't really answered my question. "I'll have the waffles too."

"Two orders of waffles, you got it."

"I'm Tracy," Tracy says, wrapping her fingers around the glass of water. "I'm Samantha's best friend."

"Hi, Tracy. Nice to meet you."

Tracy doesn't smile. She glares at Charity, and I can't say that I'm surprised she's acting so rude. I'm just wondering how far she's going to take it.

"Wait," Tracy calls as Charity starts to walk away. "I changed my mind." She looks down at the menu, squinting her eyes. "I'll have a BLT, extra tomato, add cheese and avocado, lightly toasted, no crust. A Diet Coke to drink, light on the ice, and keep them coming."

I thought we agreed to drink water to save money.

"Good choice," Charity says, nodding.

"Aren't you going to write it down?" Tracy asks.

Charity taps her finger on the side of her head. "I've got it all up here," she says like she's an old pro, and not at all offended.

So far, she hasn't done anything wrong. Charity is just the same here as she is at the hotel—way above average, practically flawless. I hate her.

Charity's eyes flick to me. "Would you like anything else to drink, besides water?"

Maybe I should splurge and just spend the money. "Diet Coke."

"You got it." Charity leaves to get our drinks and returns way too quickly. How did she do that so fast? "Here you go. Enjoy."

Tracy rolls her eyes, and I think Charity notices, but again she doesn't react.

I take a sip of Diet Coke while Tracy shoots dirty looks at Charity. Maybe it was a mistake to bring her with me. "Stop staring at her," I whisper. "You're being way too obvious."

The scowl on Tracy's face softens only slightly when she looks at me. "Samantha, I don't care if she thinks I don't like her. I don't. Just look at her. She thinks she's so much better than us. Her nose is literally up in the air. She's a snob."

Tracy is overreacting. Charity's nose isn't in the air. Charity has good posture, that's all. "Just don't go overboard, okay? Take it down a notch."

"Okay, fine." Tracy looks down at her phone instead of at Charity. That's more like it. She sucks down her Diet Coke, practically slamming the glass on the table. Then a couple seconds later, Charity drops off another Diet Coke and retrieves the empty glass.

Tracy squints her eyes, trying to see better. Then she cocks her head as Charity heads to another table. "I don't think Charity is eighteen. I bet she's a minor who ran away from home. That's why she doesn't want to be found. She doesn't have an abusive ex-boyfriend. She's lying."

Hmm. That sounds plausible. "You might be right. Maybe I should do a search for missing persons."

Tracy holds up her glass of Diet Coke, one eye squinting. "There's too much ice in here. I said light ice."

There isn't too much ice. She's exaggerating. "Well, you said to keep them coming, and that's what Charity's doing."

"I didn't come here to be polite," Tracy says, eyes blinking. "And I'm just getting started."

"What are you going to do?" She better run her plan by me first, so I can stop her if it's too extreme.

"Don't worry about it. I've got this." Tracy's eyebrows arch up into her bangs. "An ounce of prevention is all you need for a cure."

"I don't think that's how the saying goes."

"I know," she says smugly. "I changed it. I like the way this sounds better. And anyway, I know what I'm doing. Girls like Charity need to be dealt with early, before they get too comfortable—" Tracy stops talking mid-sentence and sits up taller. Charity's approaching our table with our food. "It's about time," she says loudly, placing her napkin on her lap.

The plates are set down in front of us, and Tracy immediately begins pulling apart her sandwich to inspect it.

"Anything else I can get for you?" Charity asks, smiling. Her kindness can't be genuine. It's not natural to be this happy all the time.

Tracy nudges her plate away from her. "I only see two slices of tomato. I said extra tomato. And this bacon is cold."

I watch Charity's face to catch her reaction, wondering how mad she is right now.

"I'm so sorry," she says. "Let me take care of that for you."

Wow. I didn't detect the slightest hint of irritation. She's good.

When Charity returns, she brings Tracy a small bowl of sliced tomatoes and four extra pieces of hot bacon, still sizzling. She asks us if there's anything else we need, and she's still smiling! How in the world does she do that? Is her smile sewn onto her face? Tracy had basically scolded her, called her out on being a bad waitress, yet here she is, not bothered one bit. Does she not have feelings? Is she some kind of robot that only has one mode—happy? Does she ever sweat or get nervous? She looks like she is still fresh, like she just got out of the shower. If I had been serving Tracy, I would have been intimidated by her. Tracy is the kind of girl you don't want to have as an enemy. She's tough and always has been. I've seen her beat up boys before. She's big, but not fat, more like big-boned, and she's tall.

Tracy cocks her head, pointing. Her eyes are laser focused on Charity. "My drink is empty."

Just then the other waitress swoops in and sets down a full glass of Diet Coke right in front of Tracy.

"Thanks, Sloan," Charity says to her, then she smiles at us, her green eyes sparkling. "Anything else?"

Charity truly sounds like she wants to know the answer to this question, like she's not asking us just because she's supposed to. She acts like waitressing is a satisfying and fun job for her. But it can't be. Charity is so out of place here—any casual observer could see that.

Tracy takes a gulp of her Diet Coke. "Light ice next time."

Seriously, Tracy? Could she be any more obvious? Charity is going to think that I brought Tracy here to give her a hard time on purpose, and I guess I did, but I only wanted Tracy to be a little mean, not ridiculous.

"These waffles taste pretty good," I say, as if I'm complimenting Charity, but I know she didn't make them. I'm desperate to find a way to make things less awkward. "Have you tried Veronica's waffles?" I ask. "She's a really good cook."

"Is she? I didn't know that."

Huh. I guess Veronica must not have invited Charity over to her house for a meal yet, only dessert and poker.

After Charity leaves our table, Tracy shoots me a disapproving look. "I wouldn't have told her about Veronica's cooking if I were you. Now she has an excuse to get invited over to her house for dinner, breakfast, whatever. She'll tell her that she heard about her cooking skills, and Veronica will welcome her into her home. She'll probably sit Charity next to Roy at the dinner table. Then they'll play poker after dinner. She'll stay for dessert, then maybe a movie—"

"I get it," I say, cutting her off, because I know she's right, and I don't want to envision all those things actually happening.

Tracy nods to Charity. "Girls like that don't stay single very long. You need to keep her away from Roy, or him away from her."

How? She lives and works at the hotel. I wish I wasn't so concerned about Roy falling in love with Charity. I can't stop thinking about it. "What am I going to do?"

"I don't know. We'll figure something out." Tracy stuffs a piece of bacon into her mouth as she thinks.

I turn and look out the window, and as I scan the parking lot, I notice a familiar blue pickup truck. It's back again? I've seen it here once before, when I was driving by. Well, I wasn't really driving by—that's just what I told Roy. I had actually parked here to see if Charity was working. I wasn't brave enough to come in and order anything to eat. The other time I saw this truck was in the parking lot at the hotel. I wonder what he's doing here. Why is he just sitting there?

My phone vibrates. There's a new email notification. I tap the screen and about drop my phone when I see a picture of Charity and Roy cheek to cheek, smiling for the camera, arms around each other. The next picture is even worse. They're literally one inch apart from each other, about to kiss!

When Tracy sees the picture, she smacks her glass down on the table, Diet Coke splashing.

"I've gotta get out of here," I say, scooting out of the booth.

CHAPTER 14

SPIKE

Samantha is spending the night at my house. Not *with me*—I mean, let's not get ahead of ourselves—but technically, *in* the same house. Which is huge. Because even though she's here for my sister, Tracy, there is a very realistic possibility that me and Samantha could wind up hanging out together…all night.

Everyone knows Tracy's bedtime is embarrassingly early. The girl is out cold by 9:00, like she's training for sleeping as an Olympic event. And once she's out, she's basically a log with a ponytail. There is no chance she'll be interrupting anything.

But here is the best part. No parents either. My dad is pulling the night shift down at the brewery, and my mom is visiting her sister this weekend. Boom. Cue the romantic music. This is *the* night.

Sure, Samantha's stayed over before. Plenty of times. But *this* time feels different. I think I've got a real chance with her. She has been giving me signs—several instances lately where I've caught her staring at me. She's been more touchy too, as in *her* touching *me*. Like the other day, I made a joke. She touched my arm when she laughed, and let it linger.

She used to mostly ignore me, but she's been laughing harder at my jokes and seems way more interested in talking to me—even texting me. Like, out of nowhere. Not just "Hey, is your sister home?" either. Actual conversations. Memes. Emojis. I'm serious. This is real. It's destiny.

I may or may not have doused myself in Axe. The Phoenix one. She said she liked how it smelled once, so naturally, I bought five cans. If I smell like a deodorant commercial, it's *for a reason*. I'm totally prepared to lure her in.

The house is clean. And I don't mean guy-clean, I mean *Mom would approve* clean. Kitchen? Spotless. Living room? Vacuumed. My bedroom? Basically a hotel suite—just in case the vibe magically shifts and we need a private conversation space. Or, you know, she randomly falls in love with me and needs a minute to process her feelings.

I've set the thermostat to *strategically chilly*. Not freezing or anything, but like, *blanket temperature*. And oh, look! What's this? A blanket just *happens* to be folded on the couch. Pure coincidence, obviously.

Fireplace? Ready. Wood? Stacked. Fire starter? Positioned like it's part of a heist plan. If she's craving something sweet, I've got marshmallows, graham crackers, and chocolate locked and loaded. S'mores are romantic, right? It's science.

The fridge is stocked with Diet Coke, Diet Pepsi, Diet Dr Pepper—all of her favorites. Popcorn's going in the microwave the second she says the word, maybe put on a Taylor Swift documentary—whatever she feels like watching—but fingers crossed she picks horror. Something with enough jump scares for me to be like, "Oh no, don't worry, you're safe now," and slide my arm on over.

I walk over to my desk, sit down in front of my computer, and pull up her Instagram. There she is—Samantha freaking Maxwell. The girl I've been crushing on since I was in elementary school. Man, she looks good. That smile of hers, those eyes…just melt me.

This is the night. I can feel it. After tonight, she's not gonna see me as her best friend's dorky little brother anymore. I'll be the guy who makes her laugh. The guy with the good snacks and her favorite soda. The guy with a fireplace and a warm blanket.

Yep. She's totally gonna fall for me.

My phone buzzes with a text from my friend Casey. He's out front waiting for me. He's going to drive us over to Jesse's Diner. I know Samantha and Tracy didn't invite us, but we're going to show up anyway. I just hope they're still there and haven't left yet.

When we pull up to the diner, I find Samantha in the parking lot by herself, about to get into her car. "Pull over here," I say to Casey.

"Looks like we're too late," he complains. Ha! The guy thought we were coming here to eat.

I push the door open. "We may have missed dinner, but trust me, the timing is perfect." I run across the parking lot toward Samantha. "Hey!"

"What are you doing here?" She looks past me and notices Casey. "Are you guys going inside to eat?" The expression on her face can only be described as horrified. Not what I expected. "You guys should eat someplace else. Do not go in there."

Didn't she just eat there? I thought the food was good. "Why? Is the food poisoned or something?" I laugh.

"No, it's just that…" Her eyes dart around as she hesitates. She's nervous for some reason. She and Tracy must be up to something.

"It's just that *what*?" Why doesn't she want me and Casey to eat here? What's she hiding? I turn and look back at the entrance to the diner, still no sign of Tracy.

"Just promise me you'll eat someplace else."

She's not going to get away with that kind of an answer. "Only if you tell me why." I smile at her playfully.

Samantha heaves out an irritated sigh. "Because I don't like one of the waitresses."

"Why would that affect me?"

She rolls her eyes. "Because I just don't want you around her."

I laugh out loud at her ridiculous explanation. "Why are you afraid to tell me what's really going on? Who is she? Why is it such a big deal? Is she a witch? Are you afraid she might put a hex on me?" I chuckle.

Tracy grumbles behind me. Whoa. I didn't even realize she was standing there.

"Charity might be a witch," she says with a scowl on her face. "She's definitely the type."

"A witch?" I laugh. These girls must really hate this Charity chick.

Tracy takes a sip of her soda, then stomps her foot on the ground. "I told her light ice. She filled my cup up with way too much ice! She did it on purpose—I know she did!" Tracy spins around and marches back into the diner.

I clasp my hands together like I'm pleading. "Just tell me what the deal is with this waitress."

"Okay, fine. I'll tell you." Samantha takes a deep breath, but she doesn't look like that helped to relax her at all. "I think Roy is cheating on me with her."

"Seriously?" I glance back at the diner. Now I definitely gotta go in there. I want to see what this girl looks like.

"Yeah, seriously. So just stay away from her."

I can't keep myself from smiling. There's something about seeing Samantha all jealous and possessive, it just makes me want her even more. I like it when she's feisty. "Why does it matter if I'm around Charity?"

"Because I don't want her to work her witchcraft and cast some kind of spell over you like she did with Roy."

Is she trying to protect me from this girl for my own sake, or does she want to keep me for herself as a backup for Roy? Man, I think Samantha's into me. I doubt she would admit it, but I definitely think she's hot for me.

Samantha peers up at me through her long eyelashes. Those pouty lips, I can't keep my eyes off them. Jealousy looks good on her. A breeze blows through her hair and it gets all tangled over her face. She has never been more attractive to me than right now.

I pull my phone from my pocket and hit play. Samantha looks up at me, eyes wide. Yep, I'm playing her favorite Taylor Swift song, the one she said she wished could be hers and Roy's, but Roy didn't want to pick out a song for them. He wasn't into that kind of thing.

I watch for her reaction. Will she be even sadder, realizing Roy isn't the guy for her? Or will she cheer up, feeling comforted by the song, and by me—the guy who played it for her? I take my shot.

"You want to dance?" I ask, turning the volume up and setting my phone down on the hood of her car.

"No, I don't want to dance." She doesn't sound like she has really made up her mind. I think she wants to dance with me.

"Don't make me dance to this song by myself. You know Taylor Swift deserves more respect than that." I hold out my hand, waiting for her to take it.

"Only because I don't want to disrespect Taylor," she says, placing her hand in mine. Whatever you say, I think to myself as I wrap my hands around her waist and start swaying. She places her hands around my neck and she's singing along to the song, but not loud enough for me to hear all that well. I wait another few seconds, then move in closer, pulling her against me, and she lets me. Holy crap. She is into me! Roy, you messed up, dude. Your girl is mine now.

I lean down, my mouth next to her ear. I want to kiss her so bad, but I gotta be patient. I haven't sealed the deal yet. It's too soon.

"Samantha," I whisper. "If you were my girlfriend, this would be our song."

She doesn't respond and that's okay. I just want her to think about that. She doesn't need Roy when I'm here.

Our slow dance together goes by way too fast. The song is almost over, and I definitely don't want it to end. But at least I still have tonight. Who knows what might happen?

As the final chorus plays, I pull her in closer one last time and she rests her head on my chest. Oh yeah. This girl is gonna be mine. I should thank Roy for cheating on her next time I see him.

CHAPTER 15

CHARITY (BELLANY)

Samantha and her giraffe-neck friend have finally gone. Poor girl, she's going to be feeling the effects of Ex-Lax in about six to twelve hours. I dissolved a tablet in each of her Diet Cokes and added some sugar to mask the taste. I chuckle to myself. That's what she gets for trying to mess with me.

I'm down to only one table now. Mr. and Mrs. Sims are here. They come in a couple times a week. He orders a hamburger and fries. She orders a BLT and fries. They're not all that friendly, but I think that's just their personality. Our conversations are short, no extra nonsense, not even *how have you been*, or *we've been having nice weather*. It's just stuff like *I'll have another Coke and some more ketchup.*

I suspect that he is the same Todd Sims who Veronica is paying two hundred dollars a month. Todd doesn't look like he's rolling in the dough. His clothes are plain and well-worn, and the same goes for his wife.

Today, Mrs. Sims seems quieter, more reserved, maybe even sad. She didn't order her food. Her husband ordered for her and instead of her usual, he ordered her soup.

After they finish eating, Todd comes to the register, which is also different. He usually pays at the table. I'm not sure if he's in a hurry. Maybe his wife isn't feeling well, because she has already left the diner.

I can appreciate people who like to keep to themselves, I would prefer that really. But I am curious about what's going on with them. Why is his wife acting weird today, and what is their connection to Veronica?

I take his ticket. "How was your food today?" I dare to ask, expecting the usual answer, *fine.*

He turns to look out the window at his wife, I assume, who's waiting in their car. "Lunch was fine."

What a shocker. He hands me his credit card, eyes on the counter, staring at nothing.

"How's Mrs. Sims today?"

He glances out the window again. "Yeah, she's, uh, she's not feeling the best today."

"I'm sorry to hear that. I hope she feels better soon. Maybe some soup to go might help her feel better?"

Todd shakes his head. "I don't think that's going to help with what's going on."

My curiosity is piqued even more now. "Anything I can do to help?"

He exhales, scratches the side of his face. "It's the news. Those reporters, all they do is scare people. All they're talking about is the snow melting."

Snow melting? What's so distressing about that? "Oh," I nod, but keep an inquisitive expression on my face. "So what happens when the snow melts?" *You can't make any more snowmen? You can't go skiing? What's the big deal?*

His eyes widen, and I feel like he's about to tell me some long story about ghosts and goblins or something like that. "When the mountains are packed with snow and there's a sudden change in temperature causing it to melt, it's all gotta go somewhere."

Melting snow. I see. "Is that bad?" I hand him back his credit card.

"Yeah, it's bad," he says, practically snapping at me. "Where do you suppose all that snow's gonna go? It's not just gonna disappear. It's gonna turn into water, and it's going to do exactly what it did five years ago. It's gonna flood the entire town!"

"A flood?" I repeat. "How bad does it flood around here?"

He tips his hat, eyes wild, his mind swirling with thoughts.

I'm waiting and waiting and waiting for him to answer me. *Come on, Todd. Spit it out. I don't have all day.*

"When it floods, this town shuts down. Stores, roads, houses…" he motions with his hands like he's sweeping the counter clean, "all flooded. Water everywhere. Absolute disaster and devastation!"

Okay, that actually does sound serious. "So does the whole town evacuate?"

Another distant look, he pauses in thought. "Either that, or they find someplace on high ground that doesn't flood. There's not many options. Mrs. Sims is upset because she already tried to book one of the two hotels that doesn't flood, but it's already full. We only have one other option, and Mrs. Sims doesn't want to have to stay there."

Now we're getting somewhere; two hundred dollars, what's it for? "Which hotel still has room?" I ask, already predicting he will say Veronica's.

His gray eyes narrow, lips pressed in a straight line. Todd clearly doesn't like the prospect of staying at Veronica's hotel either. "Hilltop Manor." He says the name like it's haunted or something. He points at me. "You better find yourself a place to stay when the flood comes. Don't wait until there's no place to go."

"Well, I happen to be staying at Hilltop Manor."

"You are?" he replies, surprised. Then he leans in like he's got some juicy gossip to share. I'm all ears. *Tell me what's going on, Todd.* "Stay away from Veronica. Don't talk to her, don't make eye contact, avoid her at all costs. She's a devil woman. You give her an inch and she takes the whole rope. Trouble! That's what she is."

Todd sounds certifiably insane. Maybe he smoked a little too much crack back when he was younger. Or maybe he still smokes it. "Thanks for the warning. But, do you mind me asking what Veronica did to make you think that she's a devil woman?"

"Do you have any children?"

"No."

"When you do have kids, don't let them anywhere near her!"

I shake my head, a serious look on my face. "I won't."

Todd's wallet is lying open on the counter, and I can see a picture of a little boy with brown hair, the same color as his wife's. He looks like he could be five or six, I'm not sure—I'm no expert when it comes to kids. I don't like children and have zero plans to have any of my own. "Is that your son?" I ask, wondering why I've never seen the boy before.

Todd flips his wallet shut, signs the receipt, and pushes it toward me, along with some cash. "Remember. Stay away from her."

"Got it."

He gives me one last look before he turns to leave.

Like usual, he left me a measly two-dollar tip. Gotta make sure that two hundred dollars stretches. I stuff the money into my pocket and watch him as he walks out the door and heads to his beat-up car.

Whatever Veronica did to make him hate her, apparently it has something to do with children, and more specifically that boy in the picture. Maybe I'll be able to get more information from his wife next time. She doesn't seem as crazed as he is.

CHAPTER 16

ROY

I coax Roscoe back to his bowl. When he was a pup he would eat anything, but the older he has gotten the pickier he has become. Finally he is finished. The door slams behind me as I walk out of the house. I'm on my way to the hotel when I see Samantha's car pull into the parking lot. I haven't told her yet that somebody emailed me a photo of her kissing Spike. I don't know how long she's been messing around with him or what exactly is going on. I wonder if she's here to break up with me. Or maybe she thinks she can keep seeing Spike behind my back. Ever since I saw that photo, I've been trying to decide how to handle the situation.

I make it inside before she's out of her car and take a seat behind my computer.

Samantha walks into the lobby a few seconds later. "Hello," she says, all cheerful.

I barely glance up at her. I know we have to talk, but I'm not sure how to start. "Hey."

She leans onto the counter, but I don't look up from the reservation system screen.

"I bet business is picking up," Samantha says, leaning onto her elbows, watching me type. "I wonder how bad the Chehalis River will flood. Do you think people are just overreacting or is this a real concern?"

Grandma coughs. "I've lived here all my life, so I can tell you with complete certainty that this is going to be a bad one, maybe one of the worst."

"Worse than five years ago?"

"Yep," Grandma replies and coughs again.

Samantha walks around the counter, through the doorway and into the office. She stands behind my chair, then reaches her arms around my shoulders. I keep typing while she hovers there, watching me.

It's difficult to pretend like I don't know what's really going on. The image of her with Spike is all I can think about. I really don't want her touching me right now. I get up from my chair, distancing myself from Samantha.

Grandma pops a couple cheese puffs into her mouth and flips her book open, but she's not reading. Her eyes are on Samantha. Grandma knows about the picture. She could tell I was feeling down; and she asked me what was wrong. I figured she was gonna find out anyway, so I decided I might as well tell her.

"So are you staying for dinner tonight?" She definitely sounds like she hopes Samantha will say no, and I think Samantha picked up on Grandma's unfriendly tone.

"Oh…um…" she stammers. "I'm going to spend the night at Tracy's house tonight, so I won't be able to join you. I'm kind of bummed, though, because I love your cooking."

Grandma nods, stuffs more cheese puffs into her mouth as she trains her eyes on her book.

Samantha turns to me, biting her lip like she's nervous. "I told Tracy I'd come over around five, so I've got about an hour and a half before I need to leave."

Why did she even come here at all if she's already planning on being with Spike later? How long is she going to keep up this charade?

"I was kind of hoping you could inflate the tires on my car for me," she says. "The sensor went off again. I don't know why they keep deflating. And could you also take a look under the hood, or maybe we could go to the auto supply store and have them test my battery, because there have been several days where my dad has had to jump-start my car in the morning."

Now it all makes sense. She wants to use me first. I hate that she is treating me this way. It hurts, but I'm not going to say anything. No matter what she has done, I still care about her, and I'm worried about her. With floods likely, she needs a reliable vehicle. I definitely don't want her to get stuck somewhere.

CHAPTER 17

SAMANTHA

I feel better now that I'm at Tracy's house. The last time I spent the night here, I was so upset over that photo of Roy and Charity, I almost kissed Spike, but luckily I stopped myself before it was too late. I haven't confronted Roy about the photo yet. I guess I'm just too chicken. I'm afraid when I do, he's going to use the opportunity to break up with me.

Tracy said I should dump him. She thinks I'm making a huge mistake staying together with him, and maybe I am. I don't know. I just wish Charity would leave town or disappear somehow. If that were to happen, then my problems would be solved. I'd have Roy to myself again, just like before. Or maybe it wouldn't be just like before. Maybe I'm being delusional to think that we would ever be okay again. Tracy's probably right. I should break up with him.

Wait, no. I don't want to break up with him. Ugh. I wish I knew what to do.

I feel like my whole world is falling apart; the entire town is in an uproar over possible flooding, and I'm nervous about what might happen. My dad is working up in Seattle and won't be back until tomorrow afternoon. He thinks the flood won't reach our neighborhood until late in the evening tomorrow.

Even though I'm totally depressed about Roy, somehow I'm managing to put it out of my mind. Maybe I'm just desperate to escape from reality, and I'm not thinking clearly, but I don't really care. I'm having fun with Tracy, Spike, and Casey.

I haven't played Uno since I was probably in elementary school, but for some reason I am on fire, winning almost every game. Tracy keeps laughing hysterically every time she loses. Spike and Casey are no match for me either. It's like I'm an Uno genius. Who would've thought?

I lay my last card down and shout, "Take that, losers."

Spike tosses his cards onto the table. "All right. You're cheating," he laughs. "I know you are." He snatches hold of my wrist, trying to reach inside my sleeve. "You've got cards stashed up here. That's how you're doing it."

Tracy's laughing, Casey's rolling his eyes, and I'm smiling so big my cheeks hurt. I yank my arm away and take off running. Spike's chasing me around the house. Tracy's laughing and shouting, "Get her. She's cheating!"

Spike catches me a few times, still trying to check my shirtsleeves, but each time I pull away and take off running again. When we're clear on the other side of the house, Spike finally corners me.

He's got me backed up against the counter, and I can't get away. We're standing face-to-face, out of breath from running. My stomach flutters as I stare into his deep blue eyes. My heart pounds in my chest. The thrill of being pursued, the feeling of being desired and wanted, it's all so intoxicating. I'm not thinking about running away from him anymore. I like being close to him; I like it way too much.

What happens next…happens so fast. I know what I should do; I should turn my head or push him away. I shouldn't let myself get caught up in the moment, because now, it's too late.

CHAPTER 18

CHARITY (BELLANY)

I walk through the hotel lobby door after having finished cleaning and find Roy and Veronica in the middle of a heated conversation. I knew it was just a matter of time before something like this would happen. Veronica is too much of a hothead and set in her ways to handle confrontation or stress—not to mention she's old. I'm sure it doesn't take much to upset her.

I don't feel awkward or apprehensive about having walked in on this. I think I've been desensitized to people losing their cool. I grew up in a house where it happened every day. Both of my parents constantly yelled and screamed. It often started with my mom getting after me over something stupid. My dad would jump in, and they'd wind up in a big fight.

My mom used to make a huge deal out of any flaw in my appearance.

The most infuriating part was that she never seemed to look in a mirror herself. When my dad married her she was beautiful. After they married, she really let herself go—overweight, out of shape, hair a disaster—and the way she dressed drew attention in all the wrong ways. Everything she picked apart about me was a million times worse with her.

At least my mom's bad behavior was somewhat predictable. My dad was the erratic one. He had this ability to switch back and forth from being angry to calm almost instantly. He would be yelling and carrying on, throwing things, hitting me, lost in absolute rage like some kind of monster, but if the need were to arise, like if someone showed up at the house and was knocking on the door, he could switch over to his public persona, becoming once again calm and cool. I was never physically strong enough to overpower my dad, like I could with my mom. It was easy to snatch a wooden spoon away from her or to push her back if she had pushed me. With my dad, I wasn't so fortunate.

"No!" Veronica slams down one of her books onto her desk. "It's my right as the owner of this hotel. I can refuse service to anyone at any time for any reason. I do not want that lowlife scum setting foot on this property. He can go to the local shelter at the high school if he needs a place to stay." She grunts as she struggles to get out of her chair, snatches her box of cookies, and wobbles out the door.

I raise my eyebrows, acting like I'm surprised she's upset, hoping that Roy will give me the backstory without me having to ask.

He shuts the cash drawer and sets a piece of paper in a box to be shredded. The phone rings, but he doesn't pick it up. I'm not sure if I should offer to answer it. That's not my job. I'm just the lowly cleaning lady. Answering phones is above my pay grade.

Roy still isn't speaking. I'm not sure if he's mad or embarrassed or if he's trying to figure out how to handle Veronica. I hop up on the counter, my feet dangling, and watch him shuffle through a stack of mail. "I noticed the vacancy light has been turned off," I say in an effort to start up some kind of conversation with him.

"I rented a room to someone my grandma hates. Joshua Iverson."

Joshua Iverson! That's the other guy who Veronica's been sending checks to. She sends him five hundred a month.

"I didn't know it was him on the phone until I asked for his credit card information. So now I've got to call him back and tell him I made a mistake and that the room is no longer available." Roy shakes his head. "I predict the conversation is not going to go well." The phone rings again, and Roy doesn't answer it.

"Do you want me to…" I angle my head toward the phone.

"We're completely booked. There's no point in answering."

I lean in closer to the phone, find the button to silence the ringer and press it.

"Why didn't I think of that?"

I smile. "Do you want me to call this Joshua guy?"

He tosses some of Veronica's candy wrappers into the trash. "No, I'm going to call him. And as soon as I hang up the phone with him, he'll call Mack at the campsite to reserve a spot. Mack will tell him there aren't any vacancies, but that won't stop Joshua Iverson.

He'll just join with another group at the campsite. That kind of thing happens all the time, especially during a flood. Everybody just crowds in there until the roads are completely blocked with vehicles."

"What did this Joshua guy do to make Veronica hate him so much?"

"I don't know." Roy opens a drawer and finds more food wrappers. He gathers them all up and stuffs them in the garbage.

"Any guesses?" I press.

"No."

That was a lie. Roy is avoiding eye contact with me. He's hiding something. "Why don't you ask him when you speak to him on the phone?"

Roy continues straightening up the office, throwing trash away, stacking papers. I'm not getting the reaction from him that I want. I need to come up with something else. I know. "Or..."—I pause, raising an eyebrow—"you could ask his wife or girlfriend or whoever he's with. You might get a better idea about what's going on if you talk to her instead of him."

Roy stops cleaning. He sits down and rocks back in his chair, turning a pen over in his hand, thinking.

"I have another question," I say.

"What's that?" Roy asks, still not giving me eye contact.

"If Joshua stays at the campground, what's Veronica going to do about it? Is she going to try to kick him out?"

A woman in her early thirties enters the office, interrupting us. She's looking to reserve a hotel room. Her three children are waiting for her in the car. I can see them through the window. Roy gives her the room he had originally reserved for Joshua. As soon as the woman leaves, he picks up the phone and calls to inform Joshua that he had made a mistake and the room isn't available.

While he's on the phone, I start straightening up Veronica's desk, picking up where Roy had left off since he didn't finish. I don't want him to think that I'm deliberately listening in on his conversation, even though I am.

"So the room is no longer available…" Roy says, then pauses as he listens to whatever Joshua is saying. "My name is Roy… No sir, Veronica is not here right now." Another pause. "As I explained, it was an error with our reservation system. I apologize, but we are completely full…"

As I'm stacking up Veronica's romance novels, I notice an envelope sticking out of one of them, so I flip the book open. The envelope has Veronica's name scrawled on it. I look up at Roy. His back is turned to me, so I open the envelope and slip out the piece of paper inside. It reads:

We want an additional $300 a month. The new amount will be $500. If the next check is incorrect, our deal is off, and we'll tell him the truth. You have been warned.
Todd

Mr. Sims wants more money? What kind of dirt does he have on Veronica? Who is he going to tell the truth to? I wonder if Veronica is going to pay him.

Roy sets the phone back down on the receiver, and I quickly stuff the note into my back pocket. He starts typing something, still distracted, so I quickly fold up the note, stick it back inside the envelope, and place it right back where I found it, between the pages of Veronica's book.

I didn't hear him ask Joshua about the bad blood between him and Veronica. Doesn't Roy want to know what's going on? Isn't he curious? Somehow I've got to convince him to look into this further.

I pick up a mint from Veronica's candy dish and start unwrapping it as I wait for Roy to finish on the computer. "So where can we find Joshua Iverson's wife?" I ask, then pop the mint into my mouth, waiting for him to answer.

Roy hesitates. "She works at the gas station by the freeway entrance. I see her there all the time, but only from a distance. I never go into the store. She stares at me sometimes. I can see her watching me through the window."

I raise my eyebrows and smile. "Then she knows what's going on."

More customers walk into the lobby: a young couple with a brand-new baby. The look on Roy's face when he tells them there aren't any rooms left, it's full of sorrow and sadness. He picks up the phone to call Mack at the campground to see if there's anything available. But there isn't. He even calls the other hotel to check. Nothing is available.

"Roy, can I talk to you for a second?" I say, motioning for him to step away from the counter. "They can have my room. I can stay in the back storage room. It's plenty big enough, and it's warm."

Something in the way he's looking at me right now... I don't know what he's thinking exactly, but it's like he's really taking me in, as if he's seeing me for the first time. I think I've just won him over and stolen a small piece of his heart.

What boy wouldn't fall in love with a girl like me? Not only am I beautiful, but I'm charitable, just like my name says. I have sacrificed my own comfort and convenience for someone else in need, and Roy loves me for doing it. Under normal circumstances, I would never do something generous and selfless like this, but he doesn't need to know that.

Roy places his hands on my shoulders, looking at me. His brown eyes are mesmerizing. They kind of remind me of what Quentin's looked like. "Why don't you stay at the house with me and my grandma?"

I know the exact move I should make. This is all about strategic, calculated planning. I'm gonna get what I want in the end, and he's going to give it to me. I let out a sigh. "I don't want to impose. Really, I'm fine with staying in the storage room. I'll sleep on one of the rollaways."

His fingers tighten on my shoulders, but he's still being gentle. And we're still standing very close to each other. I'm trying to concentrate and not get caught up in the moment. I don't think I've wanted someone this bad before. He is the total package: Looks, brains, money, goodness. I'm being patient and holding back the desire I have to kiss him right now. It's not easy for me to do. He should know that when he touches a girl this way, when he looks into their eyes, it makes them melt, their knees become weak. He should be careful doing that to me. I might not be quite so passive as I have been toward him in the past. I might just take advantage of him.

I know he feels the attraction we share for each other. That's why he's touching my shoulders and staring into my eyes. He wants to know what it would feel like to kiss me. I bet he's imagining it right now. I am too.

The couple at the counter start talking to each other, finally breaking Roy's stare. He lowers his hands from my shoulders, his eyes shifting back to me again. "You can't stay in the storage room," he says. "All of the rollaways are reserved, so you won't have a bed to sleep on."

"I can sleep on the floor."

He shakes his head. "There are two extra bedrooms at Veronica's house, with comfortable beds."

I want to say, *Oh really? Just how comfortable are they?* But I don't. I've got to play hard to get. "What about that cottage back in the woods? Is anybody staying there?"

"It might be a bit drafty, and I'm not sure it's been cleaned lately." He lowers his voice. "Are you sure you want to stay back there by yourself?"

"I'll be okay. Besides, if I need anything, I'll just call you." I smile.

I hope he knows what I really mean; that I want him to come over tonight. But I have to be careful. I can't be too direct with him.

Roy's phone buzzes in his pocket. When he pulls it out, I see Samantha's picture on the screen. "Hello," he says, placing his phone to his ear. He motions to the couple with the baby that he's going to be another minute.

As I listen to him talk on the phone with Samantha, my prior optimism falls flat. I can't believe what I'm hearing. He's still together with her.

My hands tighten into fists when I hear him offer her one of the bedrooms at his grandma's house. Samantha declines because her dad is supposed to be staying in the hotel room with her. But Roy isn't deterred. Again, he offers to have her and her dad stay at the house.

I don't know how this is possible, but the altered photos I sent to them have had zero effect on their relationship. These two must be closer than I thought.

How foolish of me to believe that he was done with her and that he was flirting with me. He wasn't! He's still in love with her!

What is it going to take to break them up?

I've got to rethink my plan, and I might just have to do something drastic. They've given me no choice.

CHAPTER 19

SAMANTHA

Dad calls me on the phone in a panic: "I can't get back home, sweetheart. The freeway is flooded over."

He has been working up in Seattle all week, and I told him he should come home last night, but he thought he would be able to squeeze in one more day of work. Only, I'm not sure he's really working. I think he might be at the casino.

"Get over to Veronica's," he says. "You'll be safe there." He doesn't sound all that worried, really. We stayed at Veronica's hotel the last time it flooded, and we were just fine.

The road in front of our house is still clear, but the water is creeping into the neighbor's yard across the street. The river must have risen quickly overnight. Eventually this entire neighborhood will be submerged. Last time it flooded, it took five months for all the repair work to be completed. The drywall needed to be replaced, new wiring was put in, new flooring and siding.

As soon as I hang up the phone, Spike pokes his head in the door, with Casey right behind him. "Hey. We finished moving everything from the living room upstairs. We're going to run to pick up some breakfast. What do you want?"

"I'm not hungry." I open a drawer and begin emptying it out.

"You sure?"

"Yeah, I'm fine." He hesitates in the doorway, and I give him a look. "You better hurry before they close."

"We'll be quick, and we'll come right back to finish moving the rest of the furniture."

"Thanks."

I finish packing my bags, making sure I've got everything I need.

I check my dad's room one more time. As I stand in front of the closet, my eye is drawn to the gun case on the shelf. I don't want to be responsible for my dad's gun, but I also don't think I should leave it here. Someone could easily break in and steal it while we're gone. I pick up the gun case and take it out to my car, then lock it inside.

When I'm back inside the house, I text Roy to let him know that I'll be heading over there later. Being around him for an extended period of time isn't going to be easy. I'm feeling guilty about what happened with me and Spike. I didn't just slip up and kiss him one time. I slipped up too many times for it to be considered a mistake. What I did was intentional, and I regret it.

CHAPTER 20

ROY

I roll over, blinking my eyes at the bright light. My phone is lit up with Samantha's picture. I haven't checked on her since our call last night. I hope she's okay and not stuck somewhere. I cough to clear my throat before I answer. "Hello?"

"Roy, it's me."

She sounds fine, but I still want to make sure. I haven't checked the news report yet to find out if the roads are flooding.

"Are you all right?" I rub the back of my hand over my eyes.

"Yeah. I'm good. Did I wake you up?"

I don't want her to feel bad, so I lie. "No, I'm awake."

"I just looked outside and the water's almost to the road in front of my house."

"I figured as much," I say as I throw the blankets off of me. "I really wish you would've stayed here last night."

"I know," she sighs.

"Did your dad make it home?" I ask, hoping he did.

"He's not going to be able to make it back. He said he's stuck in Seattle, which probably means he's stuck at the blackjack table trying to win back the money he's lost..."

Samantha continues to complain about her dad's gambling addiction. I feel bad that Paul has let her down again. Of all the days to be missing, today is not one of them. He should be here for her. But I guess I'm not surprised. He has left Samantha to fend for herself before.

When she was in middle school, he would leave her at home alone for days with hardly any food to eat. At least now she's old enough to take care of herself and can drive to the store to buy her own food.

I listen patiently, letting Samantha get everything out. When it feels like she is done venting, I sit up and plant my feet on the floor. "I'll come over and help you pack."

"No, that's okay. I'm mostly packed already. I started yesterday. I'm just going to finish up a couple things and then head over there later."

"Are you sure you don't need any help?" Last time it flooded, I helped her dad move all the heavy furniture upstairs. Is she just going to leave everything downstairs and let it get ruined?

"Yeah, I'm sure. The house is ready," she says.

"How did you get all the furniture moved?"

"My neighbor helped."

Why didn't she ask me? "Okay, well, I guess I'll hang up so you can finish packing. Be careful driving over here."

"I will. I'll be there as soon as I can."

The call ends and I stare at the picture of Samantha on my phone until it fades to black. I wonder if her disappearing picture is symbolic of our relationship: Here one minute, gone the next. And I wonder if it's all my fault.

I grab a towel, about to head to the shower when my phone chimes. It's a text from Samantha: I need to talk to you about something later. I know you're gonna be busy with hotel guests today, so it's no rush. Just when you have time. See you later.

The picture of her and Spike kissing flashes through my mind. I kick my dirty clothes out of my way and punch the wall.

CHAPTER 21

CHARITY (BELLANY)

'm driving Veronica's old VW Beetle, which I hate. The paint is chipping and the heater barely works, but she offered it to me as a loaner, and I couldn't turn her down. I needed some sort of transportation to get to the diner, which I can't believe is even open today.

Flashing lights shine in the rearview mirror, and my stomach plunges. I pull over to the side of the road. My heart feels like it's going to explode in my chest. My hands grip the steering wheel, palms already sweating. Calm down, I tell myself. It's nothing. They haven't tracked you down. They don't know your real identity.

My eyes travel over to my purse. Inside I have a driver's license I stole from someone named Matilda Sweeney. I swiped it from her purse at the bus station in North Carolina. The photo of her sort of looks like me, but I'm not sure if it will fool a cop.

The last time I felt this nervous was the night I hit that girl with Quentin's car. When it happened, I kept chanting in my head, *please just be a dog, please just be a dog.* But no. It was a girl. Not only was I drunk when it happened, but I had adrenaline shooting through me; the combination wasn't good. And my head was killing me. The driver's-side airbag didn't go off, and I got a huge gash just above my hairline from slamming my head on the steering wheel. Blood was dripping into my eyes. It was all over my hands. Everything I touched was painted red. As Quentin tried to revive the girl, I stood there, barely able to breathe. My heart was beating so fast, I felt like I was going to die of a heart attack.

Somehow I was able to pull myself together. I think it was an instinctual response that finally kicked in. Human beings want to survive. It's just how we're wired. I knew what I had to do. Problem was, Quentin wasn't listening. He was still panicking even though he wasn't the one who was driving drunk. It was me.

I remember scanning the road, hoping there weren't any witnesses. When I saw that the road was clear, I jumped right into drill sergeant mode, ordering Quentin around. At first he had a rebuttal to all my plans. He wanted to call the cops and tell them what happened.

I finally got him to listen to me. "Pick her up!" I yelled at him. "Take her into the trees where nobody can see!"

I'm ripped from my thoughts when I catch movement in my mirror and see the officer's face. I recognize this man. He comes to Jesse's Diner all the time.

I roll down my window. The air feels cold, and my teeth are already chattering. My whole body is shivering. I wipe the sweat from my forehead and watch him approach. Soon I can hear the gravel crunch under his feet.

Be cool, I tell myself as I take a deep breath. You can convince this cop you're Mother Teresa if you really want to. Act like you're innocent. You have done nothing wrong.

I smile as he comes to a standstill next to my window. "Hello, Officer," I say as confidently and seductively as I can muster. I know he recognizes me. I can tell by the expression on his face, only I don't think he's surprised to see me.

"Do you know why I pulled you over?" he asks. It seems like he is about to say something else when a voice speaks over his radio. He holds up his finger and steps away.

Maybe it's my anxiety over this situation, but I'm having a hard time tapping into my usually abundant supply of confidence. I'm genuinely unsure how to handle the situation. If I flirt, that will draw him in and open the door for more interactions, more scrutiny, more curiosity. If I don't flirt, he might try to give me a ticket, which would mean running my license. That would be a whole new set of problems.

"Sorry about that," he says, the chatter on his radio finally gone.

"No problem, Officer." I flash him a friendly smile, not too flirty. "To answer your question, I don't know why you pulled me over. Was I speeding?" I know I wasn't speeding. I'm not that careless.

"Your license plate is barely hanging on by one screw." He gestures to the back of my vehicle. "I wouldn't want you to lose it."

"It is? Oh gosh. Thank you for letting me know. I'll make sure I get that fixed right away."

He cocks his head. "You're a waitress at Jesse's Diner."

I'm wearing my uniform, and I'm on my way there right now. I bet he is too. I nod. "Guilty," I chuckle.

"I usually work nights and when I finish my shift, I stop at the diner for breakfast before I go home to get some sleep."

"Sounds like a good way to end the workday—or night, in your case."

"Breakfast is my favorite meal of the day."

Tell me something I don't know, I want to say. "I guess I'm just the opposite. I usually skip breakfast."

His eyes pore over me in an intense way, like he's got some sinister thoughts going through that mind of his—the kind I don't ever want to learn about. I bet he stalks girls on the regular. He probably became a cop for this very reason. In fact, I bet his daily breakfast ritual is more of a stalking routine. He's either stalking me or he's stalking Sloan.

He pats his belly, which I think he just sucked in to make it look smaller. "As you can see, I don't skip meals." He's about twenty pounds overweight. Which isn't that bad, but regardless, he's not someone I'd ever be interested in, cop or not. I have better taste.

I stare at him and wait. There's a few beats of silence, which I'm enjoying. I want him to feel awkward and uncomfortable. He pulled me over because my license plate is hanging loose, what a joke. I'll bet a thousand dollars he's the one who loosened it. I don't think he suspects me of any crime, let alone my actual past. This guy is just interested in going out with me—I'm sure of it.

He finally breaks the silence, flashing me a smile. "Have you got a safe place to stay with all this flooding headed our way?"

"I'm all set," I say, which I'm sure is a disappointment for him.

"Well, I'll be seeing you shortly…for breakfast. You drive safely, and use extra caution where you see water over the roadway."

"Always do," I say with a smile as he turns to leave.

He didn't ask for my driver's license. I'm so relieved and at the same time I'm angry that I had to even deal with him this morning. Jesse should have closed the diner today. The entire town is about to be flooded, yet he still wanted to open for breakfast this morning, probably because he wanted someone to cook his fat butt some breakfast. He's too lazy to do it himself.

CHAPTER 22

SAMANTHA

The roads are crowded with cars. Everybody's either leaving town or heading to higher ground to escape the rising flood-waters. As I drive past Jesse's Diner, I spot Veronica's VW Beetle in the parking lot. Charity must be working right now. I continue on to the next stoplight and make a U-turn. I think I'm going to pay her a visit.

When I enter the diner, Sloan leads me to a table. I feel awkward saying this and should have said it sooner. "Sorry, but could you seat me at one of Charity's tables?"

"You too," Sloan grumbles. "I guess nobody wants to have me serve them."

I ignore her complaining and follow her to a different table. "Thanks," I say as I slide into the booth. She rolls her eyes at me, which isn't surprising. I don't blame Sloan for being bitter. I bet everybody wants to sit in Charity's section. Who wouldn't want to have the prettiest waitress serve them?

A menu slips in front of my face. It's Charity. She's smiling at me, like normal. "Nice seeing you on this lovely floody day," she says in her typical friendly fashion, which also sounds royally fake. "Having a late breakfast today or early lunch?"

I don't take the menu. Tracy swears this place gave her food poisoning the last time we were here. But I was just fine, and I'm starving. "I already know what I'm going to order. I'll have pancakes and sausage."

"Excellent choice," she says, sounding way too upbeat for a day like today. She places the menu under her arm. "What would you like to drink? Diet Coke?"

I nod. "Yes."

She scans the diner, which is practically empty. There's only one other customer in here, a cop. Her eyes land back on me again. "I can't believe it's flooding everywhere. I've never experienced anything like this before. Roy said the hotel is already booked and the phone won't stop ringing."

"Yeah, people are scrambling to find a place to stay. You're going to have a lot of rooms to clean."

Charity smiles as if this is a pleasant thing for her to hear me say. "Oh, I don't mind. I love cleaning. I've always been a clean freak, ever since I was little."

Is she serious? Could she be any more perfect?

"I'll be right back with your order," she says as she spins around.

I can't believe I'm considering doing this, but the idea has been weighing on my mind ever since I spoke to Roy this morning. I just really want to know what's going on with him and Charity. If I talk to Charity first about that picture, then I'll be better prepared to talk to Roy. Maybe she'll let me know if things between her and Roy are serious, or if it was just a one-time thing, a mistake. Knowing at least this much will help me decide whether I should confess to Roy that I cheated on him too.

Charity returns with a mug and sets it down in front of me. There's a dollop of whipped cream floating on top. I assume this must be hot chocolate, but I didn't order it. She flashes a smile. "You look like you're a little overwhelmed, and I thought this might help perk you up a bit. It's my treat."

I look overwhelmed? I didn't think I had any kind of look on my face, other than suspicion and hurt. She stole my boyfriend from me. "Thanks," I say, pushing the mug away to leave room for my plate.

"Be back soon with your food."

My phone rings and Tracy's picture appears on the screen. "Hello?"

"Samantha," Tracy says, her voice tense. "You and my brother? Why? I thought you loved Roy. He was your soulmate, wasn't he?"

Spike told her? Why did he do that? Who else has he told? "It just happened," I say, feeling at a loss for words. "I didn't plan on it."

"So are you going to break up with Roy now? Because he is still your boyfriend."

"No. I made a mistake. Please don't tell Roy—"

"A mistake?" Tracy snaps. "Spike doesn't think it was a mistake. He's totally in love with you."

That's just great. Way to lay on the guilt trip. There's no way Spike could be in love with me. That's not possible. He's just in lust with me. It's purely hormones. "Spike knows I'm still together with Roy."

"Samantha!" Tracy shouts.

"What?" I'm surprised she's acting so upset. Since when is she the morality police? I go on to remind her that Roy cheated on me first. If it hadn't been for what he did, I would have never given in to Spike's constant flirting.

"So just because Roy cheated, it's okay for you to cheat?"

I don't feel good about what I've done. I wish I hadn't done it at all. "Well, yeah. It's like an eye-for-an-eye type of thing."

Tracy flips out when she hears me say this. She's lecturing me about how two wrongs don't make a right, and how I should hold myself to higher standards; basically crushing my eye-for-an-eye defense. "Look, I'm sorry," I say. "It's never going to happen again. It was a mistake."

"Are you sure about that? I don't want you to hurt my brother."

Her words hit me hard. Me, hurt him? He's the one who was pursuing me. He knows my situation. "I'm not going to hurt Spike."

She exhales heavily into the phone. "Okay, well, it's a bit late for that. Anyway, I'll see you later at the hotel."

"Right. I'll see you then."

When the call ends, I pull up my email. I've looked at this picture, I don't know how many times already; maybe a hundred, maybe two hundred. What I don't understand is how I ended up with this photo when it looks like it was taken by Charity. Her arm is extended like she's holding the camera. How did someone by the name of Super Sleuth get it? And why did they email this to me? Is Super Sleuth actually Charity?

I pull up the picture on my phone, ready to confront her the next time she comes to my table. I plan out exactly what I will say, but each time she comes near, it's like my tongue is tied. I can barely speak.

I don't know what it is about Charity, but sometimes she can be so intimidating, and frankly she's kind of scary. It makes no sense for me to feel this way. The girl is smaller than I am, by about four inches, and she probably weighs twenty pounds less. She's no match for me, physically. Yet for some reason I'm afraid of her. She gives me this weird vibe like she's all-knowing and can read my mind. She knows how to manipulate people and has managed to insert herself into Roy's life within a very short amount of time, which is quite a shocking accomplishment. I cannot let this continue.

CHAPTER 23

ROY

Every spring it floods in the Chehalis River Valley. Most years it's pretty mild, never cresting over the riverbank, but every so often, it's bad enough to damage homes and businesses. This time around I've heard conflicting reports on the news. All of the experts say it's going to be a bad one, but some are predicting the worst flood in the past century. Others say it will be similar to what we experienced five years ago. Either way, we're definitely in for some trying days ahead.

I sense that Grandma is anxious, not because we're in danger of flooding up here on the mountain, but because we'll have a hotel full of desperate, scared, and possibly angry or hostile guests. The same is true for the campground. The gamut of emotions the guests will experience is unpredictable, which means their actions and behavior will be too. We learned last time it flooded that people can lose their patience, along with common sense and decency. A fight broke out at the campground over accusations of stealing food. At the hotel, some of the guests got into the supply closet and hoarded almost all of the toilet paper.

I'm watching Grandma as she reads over the list of people who will be checking in today. She's reacting unfavorably to almost every one of them. She's rolling her eyes, groaning, cursing, mumbling. Being a lifelong resident of Chehalis, she personally knows a majority of them. She's asking me about anyone she doesn't know.

She points at another name. "Who are the Taylors? Two kids and one adult. They're here for six nights."

"I have no idea. We basically know all the same people, Grandma. If you don't know them, then I don't either."

She reaches for a bag of Hershey's Kisses and unwraps one and pops it into her mouth. Suddenly a frown forms on her face. She's glaring at the computer screen, pointing at two names. Pam and Todd Sims. I'm the one who made this reservation. I'm the one she's going to be mad at.

"What? Why did you allow them to make a reservation? They can't stay here…" Grandma starts spewing one of the longest strings of curse words I've ever heard come out of her mouth. "Mr. and Mrs. Sims?" she shouts. "I told you not to ever let them stay here!" She begins unwrapping another piece of chocolate but gets frustrated that it's taking too long and reaches for her bag of emergency

M&M's. She grabs a fistful and pops it in her mouth like an addict needing a fix, then peers at me with accusing eyes.

I realize I'm nervously tapping my pen on the counter and set it down before taking a deep breath. "I'm sorry. It's just that when Mr. Sims called, he sounded really desperate, like he was on the verge of tears. Since we had a room available, I went ahead and gave it to him."

"Roy. You know I have banned them." She pounds her now-empty fist on the desk.

"Yeah, but you never told me why. All you have ever said is that they aren't allowed to stay here."

"I'm going to call them to cancel."

I pick up the phone before she does and move it out of her reach. "It wouldn't be right to leave them without a place to stay on such short notice."

She grumbles under her breath, and I can't understand what she's saying, which I'm sure she's aware of. When she starts playing solitaire on her computer, I suspect her tantrum is over, and she has decided not to make that phone call.

Mr. and Mrs. Sims aren't the only people Grandma has banned from the hotel and campground. Joshua Iverson is the other one. But at least with him, I have a better understanding of why.

The last time it flooded, Joshua and his five-year-old son, Liam, stayed here at the hotel. That's when an unfortunate tragedy occurred. Liam disappeared. The authorities suspected he got swept up by the floodwaters and likely drowned. Joshua kept coming back here to search for his son after his disappearance, but Liam's body was never found.

At first Grandma was sympathetic toward Joshua. She felt genuinely bad for him and tried to be accommodating. Joshua showed up here day after day looking for his son. He searched the entire seventy-five acres. Then he started showing up drunk. He kept asking the hotel guests if they had seen Liam. He would show them a picture, tell them the story, and approach them repeatedly. Grandma asked Joshua to stop bothering her guests. He didn't stop. I wondered if he suspected that something else had happened to Liam, that it wasn't the flood that took him after all.

Every time Joshua was around, I would feel sick to my stomach. Seeing the hurt, the pain, and the devastation on his face. It tore me up inside. Then one day Joshua stopped showing up.

I asked Grandma what happened to him, and she said, "He's fine. He's just trying to put his life back together."

I remember right after this, she grabbed hold of my shoulders and stared at me with an intense look in her eyes. She said, "If Joshua ever accuses you of being involved in Liam's disappearance, tell me right away. Promise me you'll tell me!"

I agreed to tell her and asked her why Joshua would accuse me of being involved, and she said, "Don't worry about *why*. Just make sure that you tell me." When I asked her to explain what she meant, she got angry and told me not to ask her about it again. I did ask her a few more times after that, and always got the same answer.

Over four years have passed since Joshua last stepped foot on this mountain, and all of a sudden he wanted to come again, only this time as a hotel guest. I suspect he just wanted to escape the flood—not come searching for his son.

I would never have reserved a room for him if I had known it was him on the phone the other day. I'm kind of glad Grandma insisted that I cancel his reservation. When I spoke to him on the phone and told him I had made a mistake and we didn't have any vacancies, he said, "Oh, right. I forgot who I was dealing with. A family of liars. I should have known you would cancel on me."

As I watch Grandma now, sitting there playing solitaire, I'm wondering if she'll ever tell me how she got Joshua to stop coming around here to search for Liam. And as for Mr. and Mrs. Sims, I wonder if she'll ever tell me what happened with them. At what point will she finally come clean? Will she ever?

Grandma switches on the fan to cool herself, and some of the papers blow off her desk, scattering onto the floor. It must be a hot flash. She complains about them all the time. She's cursing again, but at least this time her anger is not directed at me.

I hop up from my chair and start picking everything up. Mixed in with her bills and receipts, I find an envelope with Grandma's name scrawled on it. I'm about to look inside it when she snatches it out of my hand.

Why doesn't she want me to see it? Is she keeping yet another secret from me? "What's in there?" I ask.

"It's nothing." She immediately sticks it into the shredder.

"Obviously it was something."

"People are just up to no good and like to meddle in other people's lives. It was nothing. Forget about it."

The humming of the shredder has stopped, the evidence is gone, and I'm left to wonder what other secrets she's keeping from me. I stare at her in all seriousness. "If you're keeping something from me that involves the hotel, the campground, or anything else, you need to tell me. How am I going to take over the family business one day if I don't know what's going on?"

She waves her hand. "No, no. It's nothing. I tell you everything about my properties." She helps herself to another handful of M&M's and picks up one of her romance novels.

I'm afraid Grandma might get herself into trouble one day, and I won't know what to do or how to help her, because she won't tell me the truth. While this is frustrating and infuriating, I don't want to argue with her right now. I've got other more important things to take care of. All of the stores will be closing soon, and the streets will be flooded over. I pick up the grocery list that she made earlier. "I'm heading to the store. Is there anything else you want me to pick up while I'm out?"

"Let me think." Grandma gazes at the floor. "Yes, there is something. Stop and pick up some more ammo for the rifles, just in case our hotel guests get out of hand. I don't know half of these people, and I haven't forgotten that Charity's ex-boyfriend is trying to track her down. If there's trouble, the sheriff may not be able to get to us. We need to be prepared."

She's right about that. We do need to be prepared. "All right. I'll be back soon."

"Roy," Grandma calls as I'm about to walk out the door. "Buy another bag of food for Roscoe. Oh, and before you leave, go check on him in the house. I'm not sure if I filled his water bowl."

"You've got a whole closet full of dog food," I say, pointing down the hall. "He's a tiny dog and he barely eats anything."

"Just get him some more," she snaps.

"Fine."

I'm about to walk across the property toward the house when I catch sight of a blue pickup truck. It's parked across the street, and there's someone sitting inside. I wonder if this is the same guy Samantha saw lingering around town.

As I head toward the truck, I can hear its engine running. The guy behind the wheel acknowledges me with a head nod and rolls down his window. "How's it going?" he asks.

"Is there something I can help you with?"

He tugs the bill of his ball cap down over his eyes slightly. "I heard there was a campsite around here. I'm looking for it."

I want to ask him if that was really what he was doing, but I don't. I peer around the inside of his truck. It's packed full of camping gear: a sleeping bag, a couple backpacks, some duffel bags, blankets. There's an ice chest behind his seat. His truck and his gear have seen better days. The clothes he's wearing are worn too. I don't think he's much older than I am. The hair sticking out of his ball cap is blond, and it doesn't match the brown in his beard. Then I catch sight of something else in his truck and my entire body stiffens. Sticking out from under a pillow on the seat next to him, I see the grip of a handgun.

"The campsite is full," I tell him sternly. This guy better turn his truck around and drive back down the mountain right now.

His dark eyes shift over to the hotel. "Is the hotel booked too?"

"Yes."

He makes a face like he's disappointed. "I'm kind of running out of options. I can pay extra." He reaches into his pocket and pulls out a wad of cash.

"It's not a matter of money. We're full. If I were you, I'd head toward Portland."

"Portland. That's a bit far."

"It's either that or take a swim in the floodwater."

He chuckles, but I wasn't joking when I said that. "Is it really going to flood that bad?" he asks with another laugh. "Or is that just fake news?"

His smile remains even though I'm glaring at him. "Get off this mountain and go back to wherever you came from."

He holds up his hands in mock surrender, still gripping the cash. "I didn't mean to offend you. I'll be heading out. Don't worry." His tone is not apologetic.

I turn and head back across the street. The truck takes off, tires squealing. He drives into the hotel parking lot to turn around, then speeds off down the hill.

When I drive into town, my first stop is to pick up ammo. I call Mack at the campsite and tell him to keep an eye out for this guy and his blue Ford pickup truck with Virginia license plates.

CHAPTER 24

SAMANTHA

I am surprised to find that the ATM isn't working. I can check my balance, but it won't let me withdraw cash. I've never seen this before. I go to the only open grocery store in town. It's a madhouse in the parking lot and inside. Most of the shelves look bare. People are buying anything that isn't nailed down. Not a single loaf of bread remains, but I manage to snag a bag of tortillas and some other snacks.

Before I head to the hotel, I decide to fill up my car with gas since it's almost empty. As I turn off the main road, I'm overwhelmed with dread and frustration when I see the long lines of cars waiting to pump gas. I guess I'm going to be here for a while. I really shouldn't have procrastinated all of these errands.

My day has not gone at all how I planned, and I still don't know what's going on with Roy and Charity. The stress is getting to me. I'm feeling anxious.

My phone rings, and I'm surprised to see it's Veronica. Since when does she call me? This must be important. "Hello."

"Samantha, you can pick up your key at the front desk."

"Great, thanks, but I already know the combination."

"No, dear. I'm leaving you a room key. You won't need to stay at my house after all."

"But I don't mind staying at your house. In fact, I'm looking forward—"

"Lucky for all of us," she interrupts, "I had a cancellation and got you into a room at the hotel."

I'm disappointed to hear this. I really wanted to stay in the house with Roy. "Oh, okay." I didn't think it would bother Veronica to have me stay at the house, but apparently it does. She hangs up without saying goodbye, and I toss my phone onto the front passenger seat, frustrated.

The line of cars in front of me finally disappears, and I pull up to the gas pump. While I'm filling up, I watch the people around me. They're all in a hurry, just like me.

The door to the convenience store opens, and I catch sight of Charity inside. I hadn't noticed Veronica's VW, not until now. It's parked in one of the parking spaces. I wonder what she's talking to that cashier about.

I leave my car while it's still filling and head inside the store. Charity doesn't see me come in since her back is to me. I turn down the aisle toward the soda machines and start filling up a large cup with Diet Pepsi, while simultaneously trying to listen in on her conversation.

The cashier is shaking her head. "I don't know why Veronica hates my husband," she says. "Whatever happened between them, it happened years ago, before I ever got involved with Joshua."

"You don't have any idea?" Charity asks. "No theories? Nothing?"

The cashier glances around, and I slip back behind the rack of potato chips. "Joshua's son, Liam, disappeared during the last big flood. It happened at Veronica's hotel, on her property."

I swallow hard, remembering when it happened. Dad and I were staying at the hotel too. Everybody was searching for Liam for days, but he was never found. Liam's dad was so distraught, an absolute wreck. I wonder if he blamed Veronica since it happened on her property. But it wasn't her fault. It was Joshua's fault. He wasn't watching Liam, and Liam wandered off.

I had heard rumors around town that Joshua Iverson suspected something else had happened to his son—that it wasn't the flood that took him. But at no time did it enter my mind that he would ever accuse Veronica of being involved. Veronica is an old lady who only cares about her hotel, her grandson Roy, and making money. There's no way she could've been involved in Liam's disappearance.

I peek through the gap in the aisle again, wondering why Charity wants to know about Joshua Iverson and Veronica.

"That was such a tragedy," the cashier says. "I had just moved here when it happened. I remember how shook the entire town was over that boy's disappearance."

Horns begin honking outside the convenience store. Crap! They're probably honking at me. Both Charity and the cashier turn and look as I set my drink on the counter. "Hey," I say, trying to act casual. "Just this drink, that's all." I pull out my bank card and stick it into the card reader.

I think Charity is still staring at me. She must know I was eavesdropping. Either I'm really bad at playing it cool, or she's just way too good at reading people—way beyond normal human ability. If, and I mean if, aliens do exist, my finger would point right at Charity. She seems like she doesn't belong—not only in the state of Washington. She doesn't belong on this planet.

When I manage to gather up enough courage, I turn to look at her. She's smiling at me. I smile back, an apology on the tip of my tongue. Why am I about to apologize? Snap out of it. Act cool. Say something—anything. "Are you filling up Veronica's car with gas?" I ask.

A slight smirk forms on her perfectly shaped and glossed lips. I swear she wants to laugh at me right now and make me feel even more like an idiot. "Yep, all filled up."

My attention shifts to the cashier. Her name tag reads Donna. She's watching me and Charity like we're two cats about to fight. She's leaning back slightly, eyes bouncing back and forth between us.

I take the receipt from her and then pull the wrapper off of my straw and stick it through the lid. "Thanks," I say, turning to head out the door. More cars are honking. I walk quickly with my head down, trying not to look at all the angry eyes glaring at me. I feel bad for making people wait.

Before I drive off, I glance over my shoulder to make sure the path is clear of any oncoming cars, and my breath catches. It's him again: the guy in the blue pickup truck. He must have followed Charity here. If this is her ex-boyfriend, then I want to talk to him and hear his side of the story, because I have a feeling that Charity's been lying. I don't think he has done anything to harm her. I think she's done something to him.

My foot stomps on the gas as I try to catch up to him before the light turns red.

CHAPTER 25

ROY

The official hotel check-in time isn't until four, but guests are arriving early. Grandma and I haven't had a break in over an hour. I told her many times before that we needed extra help running this place, but she insisted we could handle it. The door swings open again, and more people come spilling into the lobby.

I'm seeing a lot of familiar faces and some I don't recognize at all, which is what I expected. Some of the guests aren't all that talkative. They just want their key and directions to their room. Others are acting like this is some kind of luxury vacation destination. *Is there a pool? A hot tub? A game room?* My answer to these questions is, *No, no,* and *no.* People have asked about staying in a room with a view. I tell them that each room is equipped with a picturesque view of endless trees that dot the mountainside, and if they're lucky they'll see some wildlife.

The next guest approaches the counter—a woman in her mid-forties. She sets down her oversize purse and begins pulling things out and setting them on the counter: a phone, a water bottle, some makeup, and finally her wallet. She leans in close, peering over the counter at me. "Is there a workout room? And what are the hours it's open?"

I gesture to the windows in the lobby. "The great outdoors, that's our workout room. It's open twenty-four hours a day, seven days a week. There are several hiking trails with signs posted to help guide you."

She picks up her bottled water and takes a drink as she turns to look out the windows. Then she hands me her credit card. "That sounds good. But what about weight machines? Is there anything here like that?"

This isn't the Marriott, I want to say. "There's a horseshoe pit. People enjoy throwing those. It might be a good upper-body workout. You can also chop some wood."

She arches an eyebrow at me. "I've never chopped wood. I bet it's a great workout."

"Just be careful. If you need any help, let me know."

She smiles at me, and the wrinkles under her eyes crease. "I might just take you up on that offer. I bet you chop wood all the time, don't you? I can tell by those amazing-looking shoulders you have."

I'm typing her information into the computer, hoping she won't turn out to be too annoying. Maybe I should hide that ax.

After the woman leaves, a younger man, probably in his

mid-twenties, steps forward. He's wearing boots, a vest, and a bolo tie. "Howdy," he says, tipping his cowboy hat. I nod in response, and his attention quickly shifts over to Grandma's desk behind me. It's piled with papers, food wrappers, bags of chocolate, and soda cans, most of them empty.

His blue eyes slide back to meet mine. "Name's CJ. I have a reservation."

I type in his name and pull up his information. After I review the cost of his room with him, he opens up his wallet and pulls out cash.

"We prefer credit cards," I tell him.

He scratches the side of his face and chuckles. "I thought that might be a problem, but I'm kinda stuck between a rock and a hard place, you know what I mean, friend? You see, my wallet," he pauses and takes a breath, "my original wallet was stolen. I picked this one up at the dollar store and luckily made it to the bank for a cash withdrawal before they closed. If I had a credit card, I'd give it to you, but I had to cancel all my cards. You understand, don't you?"

I'm not going to be quick to give in just yet. There are plenty of other people waiting for a chance to stay here who have credit cards. If this guy damages any property or takes off owing us money, we'll have no way to charge him for those expenses. We need to have a credit card on file.

He flashes me a sad attempt at a million-dollar smile, which has zero effect on me. "Come on, man. I promise you won't regret this. All I want is a dry place to stay."

I know he's desperate, but so is everybody else, and he's a

complete stranger. I don't know who he is, where he came from, what he's up to.

"Look," he says, leaning in closer, voice low. "I'm down on my luck, and I don't think much else can go wrong, to be honest with you. First I'm robbed, now the flood." He presses his hands together like he's praying. "You can trust that I will take great care of this here fine establishment. I have no interest in causing you any trouble. I'm a good person, I promise you—"

I hold up my hand to stop him from rambling. "I'll take cash, plus a two-hundred dollar deposit."

"Thank you. Thanks for letting me stay here. I do appreciate it. You have no idea how much this means." He shuffles through his cash, counting it out, then hands it to me. "This place looks real nice. It's got that mountain cabin feel. I'm glad I listened to Charity's advice. She told me I should come stay here."

I pause, losing count of the money he just gave me. "How do you know Charity?"

"I met her at Jesse's Diner. She's really nice. And pretty."

I give him a hard stare as a sort of unspoken warning, trying to decide if I should hand this money back to him and kick him out.

"Oh, hey…" He holds up his hands in an attempt to act innocent. "Is Charity your girl? I do apologize."

My stare remains fixed on his face. I don't trust this guy.

The phone rings, and Grandma answers it. "What's the problem?" she asks.

I don't have time to mess with this guy. I hand him his room key.

He stuffs it into his pocket and picks up his bag, slinging it over his shoulder. "You won't regret this, man."

Grandma sets down the phone and sighs heavily, rolling her eyes. "Can you go to room 116? They're having trouble with the TV."

"You want me to go now?"

"Yes, I can handle this. Just go take care of it."

I grab some extra batteries in case the remote control needs new ones and head out the door just as Charity is about to come in. She's got two gigantic fountain sodas, one in each hand.

"Thirsty?" I ask her.

She smiles and walks through the door as I hold it open for her. "One of these is for Veronica." She turns around to face me. "Where are you headed to? Do you need help with anything?"

"No, I'm good. It's just a TV emergency."

She laughs. "Sounds serious."

"Yeah, it is. They've called twice in the last twenty minutes."

"Well, don't let me keep you."

I head down the walkway exactly as the rain starts to pick up. Sure, why not, I think to myself. Just more water to add to the already overflowing rivers. A clap of thunder booms, and I look up at the gray sky. That can't be good. We usually don't get a lot of thunder and lightning.

CHAPTER 26

CHARITY (BELLANY)

I set down one of the sodas in front of Veronica. "It's Dr Pepper," I tell her.

"Thank you, hun. Can you watch the front desk while I go to the bathroom? If somebody comes in, just have them wait for me. I shouldn't be long."

"Sure, no problem," I say as I look around the empty lobby to confirm nobody else is in here.

"You holler if you need anything."

I smile and watch her hobble down the hallway. When I hear the lock on the bathroom door click, I set my soda down and run over to her desk, taking advantage of the opportunity to do some snooping around. The only thing that looks neat on her desk is her stack of romance novels. I pick up the top one and pull out the envelope she had wedged between its pages. I'm in luck. It hasn't been sealed yet.

Inside I find a check written out to Joshua Iverson. My conversation with his wife at the gas station earlier was very informative. I had no idea that this man had lost his son. I still don't know what it has to do with Veronica, though. I look at the numbers written on the check. Five hundred dollars. Yep, just like I saw on her bank account. Why is she giving him money? What really happened to his son? This has got to be hush money. I bet he found out his son didn't die because of the flood, and somehow he's holding Veronica responsible.

I flip through the pages of her book and find another envelope. This too has a check inside made out to Todd Sims in the amount of two hundred dollars. Oh. Hold on. There's a note inside here too. It reads:

Todd,

Two hundred a month is the amount Pam and I agreed on. I'm not going to give her a single penny more. DO NOT ASK ME FOR MORE MONEY EVER AGAIN!

Veronica, my dear, you are a feisty one.

So Mrs. Sims is the one who agreed on the amount of blackmail money. Her husband must be the go-between, just the messenger.

I fan myself with the envelope, wondering how Veronica got herself into this mess. Why is she shelling out a total of seven hundred dollars a month to Mr. and Mrs. Sims and Joshua Iverson? What kinds of secrets is she keeping? Veronica is supposed to be a sweet little old lady, a business owner, and a respected member of the community. But apparently she's not. I bet she's done some pretty scandalous things in her past. Did she steal money? Did she bribe someone and get caught? Did she commit some other crime? I have so many questions and zero answers. The only thing I do know for sure is that Veronica does not want Roy to find out about these checks. He has no idea that his precious grandma isn't who she seems.

I turn the book over in my hand, looking at the cover, which is a picture of a man with no shirt on and bulging muscles. He's cute but not my type. I prefer a guy with more of a rugged look. This guy is way too pretty.

I chuckle to myself, still examining the book. Veronica is a smart one. This is the perfect place to hide blackmail money from Roy. He wouldn't be caught dead looking through any of her smutty books.

The toilet flushes, and I quickly return the book to the pile. I grab the feather duster from the cupboard and head over to the counter, pretending like I've been busily dusting the whole time she's been gone.

Veronica groans as she hobbles back to her desk. Her feet barely lift off the floor. It's as if she's got cinder blocks tied to the bottom of her shoes. She glances up at me with her beady dark eyes, grimacing. "My arthritis is acting up again." The chair squeals as she sits down. The extra girth that hangs loose on her upper arm jiggles when she reaches for a bottle of ibuprofen. "Of all the days to be in pain, today is not one of them. This has been our busiest day of the year, no doubt about it. The only other time we're ever fully booked is during the Seattle to Portland bike ride."

The hotel lobby door swings open and in walks Roy. His broad shoulders fill out his flannel shirt quite nicely, and his well-worn jeans hang from his hips just right—not too tight and not too loose. Put a picture of Roy on the cover of a book, and I'd definitely buy it.

He holds the door open for a family of three coming in behind him. He welcomes them like they're old friends and reaches down to muss up the boy's hair, promising to give him a lollipop. I reach for the jar on the desk and grab two root beer–flavored lollipops—the best flavor in the bunch—and hand them to Roy. He smiles at me, and I of course smile back. Yeah, I think today is going to be full of surprises for Roy. This day will mark the point in time when his future changes course forever. Because he's going to be with me.

After Roy delivers the lollipops, I keep an eye on him as he heads down the hallway toward one of the storage rooms. This feather duster is proving to be a helpful tool today. I continue to dust off the shelves and the end tables while I wait for him to return. When he finally does, he sits down in a chair behind the counter and leans back, raking his fingers through his damp hair.

I return to the office area to be near him, even though I have already dusted in here. "So the TV crisis has been taken care of?" I ask.

Veronica's chair squeals as she leans back, her attention now on

Roy. "What was wrong with it?" She picks up her Dr Pepper and takes a drink.

"The batteries were missing from the remote."

Veronica sets down her Dr Pepper and grabs the bottle of ibuprofen again. "These people are all thieves. I should charge them extra." She pops a pill into her mouth and washes it down with some more Dr Pepper.

I ignore her comment and turn my focus back to Roy. "You're a handy guy to have around," I say teasingly.

Roy is staring at me, kind of zoned out. I'm dying to know what's going through his mind. I doubt it has anything to do with those missing batteries. There's something heavier weighing on him. The look on his face, it's almost like he's trying to make a decision about something. I wonder if it has anything to do with me. Actually, I think it might since he's staring at me.

Do I need to help him with his internal dilemma somehow? Maybe I need to do a better job at conveying my interest in him. I might not have made it clear enough. If that's the case, then I need to correct it quickly. I want Roy to feel secure when considering a future with me. I want him to know that I am interested in much more than being a coworker. I want him to know that I find him irresistible.

He rises from his chair. The distant look on his face is still there. "I'm going to drive down to the end of the road and check out how high the water is."

I open a cupboard and quickly toss the feather duster inside. "Oh, I'm curious about that too. Can I come?"

"Yeah, sure," he says with a shrug.

This is perfect. A little alone time will do us a lot of good. I'll ask him a bunch of questions about the flood, make him feel like he's smarter than me so he won't be intimidated. I'll act scared and concerned so he'll want to console and comfort me. Whatever I do and say, it's going to be for the purpose of helping him to realize that I need him, I want him, I trust and rely on him. He is my protector. Guys eat that stuff up; it really helps to boost their egos.

"Charity," Veronica calls as I'm about to walk out the door, and I swear she sounds just like my mom. She has that exact same tone to her voice. I already know she's going to ruin my plans, and I'm going to have to let her. This isn't going to be easy for me. I can already feel the anger and rage starting to fester inside me.

"Hun," she says. "You're going to have to stay here. Room 110 needs more towels, and room 111 needs another pillow."

Towels and pillows? I hardly think that's an urgent matter.

"Can't she do that when she comes back?" Roy asks.

Veronica pulls a face. "No, she can't. I have other things I need her to do too." She flicks her hand dismissively. "Dusting in here is not a priority."

Hold on a minute. She's criticizing me? What else does she want me to do? I can't clean hotel rooms when the guests are in them, and the empty rooms are already clean.

She picks up a Hershey's Kiss and begins tearing the wrapper off while her eyes remain fixed on me. "The refrigerator needs to be cleaned out in the break room. All of the expired food needs to be trashed. The same goes for the food in the cupboards and in the pantry. Any expired, stale, half-eaten food needs to be thrown away." She pauses to stick a Hershey's Kiss into her mouth, rolling the empty wrapper between her fingers. "The table in the break room is piled high with groceries that Roy picked up earlier. He already put away the stuff that needed to be refrigerated, now everything else needs to be put away."

Roy rakes his hand through his hair, grumbling. "I can help put that away—"

"You have other things to do," Veronica cuts him off.

I think I know what's going on here. She is deliberately running interference. She doesn't want me spending time with Roy, especially if we're going to be alone together. Her outrageous demands have nothing to do with work responsibilities. This old hag has decided that she doesn't like me. It's so obvious. She's going to do everything she can to make my job and existence here miserable and intolerable. She's going to try to force me out and get rid of me. Well, I have news for her. I'm not going anywhere.

"Sure thing," I say calmly. "I'll take care of it right away." I turn to Roy. "Maybe I can go with you later?"

"I think Roy's going to be busy with responsibilities here," Veronica interjects, the sound of her voice yet again reminiscent of my mom.

It's truly a miracle I'm holding it together and managing to force a smile onto my face. What I really want to do right now is take that straw she's drinking out of and stab her in the eye with it.

Roy heads out the door, keys in hand. He doesn't even look back at me. Why does he let Veronica boss him around like that? Why doesn't he ever stand up to her?

Veronica picks up the Dr Pepper I bought for her and drinks it while she's staring at me. The satisfied look on her face is oozing with arrogance, authority, and entitlement. My mother used to look at me that same way, especially after she hit me with her wooden spoon.

"Do you have a question?" she asks.

Pull it together, I tell myself. Don't give her the satisfaction of knowing that she's upset you. "No. I'll make sure to take those things to the hotel guests right away, then I'll get started in the break room."

Veronica doesn't respond. She's no longer looking at me. She's playing solitaire, purposely ignoring me.

I've made up my mind. The two of us cannot coexist. Something must be done to restore balance again around here. One of us has to go, and it's not going to be me.

As I stand in front of the supply closet, staring at the enormous amount of dog food Veronica has stashed in here, a new thought enters my mind. It's not just the dog food that has sparked this idea, it's also the story of the boy who disappeared the last time it flooded. The ideas continue to collect in my mind as I close my eyes and envision how it will all play out. I can see it so clearly.

A sudden rush of adrenaline sends a cold chill through my entire body. Everything I want, it's all within reach, ready for me to take. The power, the control, it's all coming back to me. Tonight is going to be the perfect storm.

CHAPTER 27

ROY

The road is still clear and more hotel guests have just arrived, but part of me wishes the road had already flooded, because Spike just walked in with Tracy and their dad. The picture of Spike and Samantha together is back in my mind again, and I can't stop seeing it.

Tracy leans against the counter. "Thanks for finding space for us."

"Sure. Of course." I actually didn't do them any favors. They just lucked out and reserved their rooms before they were all gone.

As soon as I hand Tracy's dad their room keys, he turns to Spike and directs him to start unloading their truck. Tracy shifts over, taking her dad's spot. "Is Samantha here somewhere?"

I've been so busy with other things, I hadn't stopped to think about Samantha. "I'm not sure. Veronica might have already checked her in." I look Samantha's name up on the computer. "It says she's checked in." I wonder why she's not in here with me right now? Is she trying to avoid me?

"Which room is she staying in?"

"She reserved the room next door to you and Spike, room 100."

Tracy frowns. "Are you sure she's checked in? I've been trying to get ahold of her on the phone, and her car's not in the parking lot. I'm kinda worried maybe she got stuck somewhere. The roads are starting to flood." She shakes her head. "I warned her to be careful. I told her not to drive over high water under any circumstances. Even the smallest amount of water can lift a vehicle and carry it away."

I pick up my phone to check for new messages. There aren't any; just that last text from this morning, saying that she needed to talk to me.

Did her car break down? Did it get swept up in the flood? I tap the screen of my phone to call her. It goes straight to voicemail. I send her a text. She doesn't reply.

Tracy and I both leave messages asking her to contact us right away. Guilt continues to swell inside me. I haven't been checking up on Samantha like I should have, and now she's missing. She's by herself, and I don't know what kind of trouble she might be in.

When Spike returns, Tracy informs him that we still can't get ahold of Samantha.

"When was the last time you saw her?" I ask Tracy.

"I saw her this morning at her house," Spike replies.

What was he doing at her house this morning? Was he there when I spoke to her on the phone?

"I was with her last night too," Spike adds as if it isn't a big deal. "She said she was going to go to the store today and get some gas in her car... I think that's about it."

Tracy giggles nervously. "Samantha spent the night with *me* last night, and Spike and Casey helped her pack up her house this morning."

The thought of Samantha and Spike together sends my thoughts down a road I'd rather not be on, because no matter which path I take, I end up in the exact same place. A future without Samantha.

I hand Tracy a key to Samantha's room. "Can you go check and see if she's there?"

"Of course I can." She hooks her arm around Spike's. I can hear her chastising him as they walk away.

I continue to check in more hotel guests, but my mind is focused solely on Samantha, my emotions bouncing all over the place. I can't let myself be angry with her, and I don't want to feel betrayed either. How can I be so selfish right now? She's missing, and she might be in trouble. I hope this isn't my fault. Could I have done something differently? Did I drive her away?

When Tracy and Spike return, they're out of breath like they've been running.

"Her stuff is in her room, but she's not there," Tracy gasps. "We searched the entire grounds of the hotel. There is no sign of her."

I leave Grandma to handle the hotel guests while the three of us run over to the house to check for her. We search the entire inside and out, then we search through the sheds and the garage. But we don't find her.

I pick up my phone and call her father. It goes straight to voicemail.

Tracy's pacing back and forth. "Her dad's still in Seattle, or at the casino, or I don't know. He has no idea where she is."

Spike gestures toward the hotel parking lot. "I've got the keys to my dad's truck. I'm going to go look for her. Do you want to come?"

My phone rings just as I'm about to respond. It's Grandma. Our conversation is brief. She needs me to get back to the hotel. She sounded overwhelmed and tired. Her health is another huge concern of mine. She's too old to run that place by herself.

When Spike hears that I'm not going with him, he gives me this look like he thinks I've got my priorities messed up. He's judging me for putting my grandmother's needs above my girlfriend's. This isn't easy for me, and I'm not happy that I have to make a choice here.

I don't know where Samantha is. I hope she's okay. Of course I'm worried about her, but I can't leave and start driving around town searching for her. If I get cut off from the hotel and I'm not able to get back, I think Grandma would literally have a heart attack. The only other person here to help her is Charity, and she's busy running around the hotel helping the guests.

Tracy twists a strand of her hair around her finger, biting her lip like she wants to say something.

"What?" I ask.

"Are you sure you can't go help look for Samantha?"

"If I could, I would."

"Liar," Spike snaps. He continues to mumble as he walks off, adding a few choice words loud enough for me to hear.

"What did you say?" I yell. *Say it again—I dare you!*

Tracy grabs Spike by the arm. "Come on, Spike. Let's go." She manages to keep him walking, lengthening the distance between us.

It takes every ounce of self-control I have inside me to keep myself from going after him.

I'm about to round the corner and head to the lobby again, when I hear Tracy calling, "Spike! Come back here!"

I spin around and see Spike charging toward me. My hands ball up into fists. The words of my grandfather come racing through my head: "If you're going to fight with someone, make your first punch count—strike hard and fast. You can always show mercy after you've established control over your opponent, not before."

Spike stops short and jabs his finger in the air. "What do you want me to say to her, huh? When she asks me where you are, should I tell her that you don't care about her, that you're too much of a coward, that you're afraid of the flood…"

My phone rings in my pocket, and I know it's Grandma calling again, wondering what's taking me so long. I don't have time to deal with Spike right now. I've gotta calm down and just walk away. I turn to leave, but Spike keeps running his mouth. He won't shut up.

"What do you want me to say to her?" he shouts louder. "That you're busy with Charity?"

All of the control, all of the patience I had left inside me is suddenly gone. There's nothing left to keep me grounded. I'm falling into a dark abyss filled with nothing but rage. I spin around, and my fist lands with a loud thud. Spike stumbles backward, and Tracy screams. She rushes to his side. Spike's standing there with his hand over his eye.

"You didn't have to hit him!" she shrieks. "He wasn't trying to fight you. I can't believe you did that!"

She's wrong. If I hadn't hit him, he would have taken the first swing. I'm not going to waste my time feeling guilty about what I did.

Charity suddenly appears, seemingly out of nowhere. I don't know how much she overheard or what exactly she saw.

"Go to the office," she says calmly. "Your grandma is waiting for you. She's having trouble with the computer program."

Before I walk away, I stare down Spike one last time. He doesn't say anything to me. He's still holding his eye. It's his fault I hit him. I'm sure he knows this.

Once I'm inside the hotel, I get to work on the computer, trying to fix the glitch or whatever the problem is. With Grandma, there's no telling what she did to cause this.

When Charity enters the hotel lobby, she heads straight to the break room and returns a few seconds later with an ice pack. She gives me a look as she walks by, and I swear she's trying not to laugh or at least not let herself smile too big. Apparently she approves of the way I handled Spike.

Grandma points at my knuckles as I'm typing on the keyboard. "What happened? You're bleeding."

"It's not my blood."

She saddles her hand on her hip. "Do I need to kick one of these guests out?"

I know she's serious and will follow through with her threat. But it's not necessary. I shake my head. "I took care of the situation."

"If anybody, I mean *anybody*, gives you any more trouble, they're out of here!" She points her thumb over her shoulder. "I'm not going to put up with any nonsense..."

Grandma continues ranting in front of a long line of hotel guests. There's nothing they can do, though. It's not like they can cancel their reservations and leave. They're stuck here with this mean old lady and a guy who beats people up. I'm sure that's what they're all thinking.

I'm so hyper-focused on the screen in front of my face that I don't notice Charity has returned until I've fixed the problem and gotten the program running again. When I get up from the chair, I'm caught off guard by her expression. She's smiling at me like I'm some kind of hero. But she's wrong. I'm not the hero. I'm the villain.

CHAPTER 28

SAMANTHA

I'm following the blue pickup truck with a Virginia license plate up the mountain, surprised it's not going to the hotel where Charity is staying. It's heading along the road that leads to the campground Veronica owns. But I guess this makes sense too. Staying at the campground as opposed to the hotel is probably a good choice. It's still close to Charity, yet not close enough for her to see him. Which I'm sure is what he wants.

I'm careful to keep my distance as he approaches the campground entrance, except he doesn't pull in, he keeps driving up the mountain right past it. I'm familiar with this road and know that it leads to a dead end. He's either going to park on the side of the road like the rest of the cars here or eventually make a U-turn and come back. It's better that I just wait here, since my Mustang can blend in with the other cars, and it'll be less obvious that I'm following him.

I slow down, about to pull over, when suddenly the truck veers off the road. It's driving down a path that's mostly overgrown with weeds. I had forgotten about the back entrance to the campground. This guy must be trying to avoid Mack, the old man Veronica hired to run this place.

Mack can be a bit intense. He's uptight and hard to get along with. He doesn't mind if music is being played too loud, but if it's the kind of music he doesn't like, he might just kick you out. If someone is having a party and people are getting drunk, being loud and acting obnoxious, Mack will let that slide if he has been provided with a generous gift of alcohol as a bribe. I heard that the last time it flooded, he limited the number of vehicles he would allow inside the campground. He made people park along the road and haul their gear in by foot.

Instead of following the pickup truck in my car, I pull over and park. There's no way my Mustang will make it down that overgrown dirt road. It's too low to the ground and will definitely get stuck in the mud.

My car door slams shut, and I start down the path on foot. While I can no longer see the truck, I'm not too concerned. I should be able to find it. This road isn't that long.

The rain is coming down hard, and I think I see a flash of lightning rip across the sky. I listen for the thunder to follow, only it doesn't come. The lightning must be too far away. I adjust the hood of my coat, pulling it lower to keep the rain off my face. Luckily I'm wearing my good raincoat that actually repels water. I should be able to stay warm and mostly dry.

I pull my phone out from my pocket to text Tracy. She's going to freak when she finds out what I'm doing. Yep, I'm about to discover the real story behind the mysterious Charity, straight from the source. My finger presses the button, but it won't turn on. Crap! The battery must be dead. I guess I won't be telling her after all. She's probably busy getting herself settled into her hotel room anyway, and I'm sure Roy is busy checking in hotel guests. They shouldn't worry about me, not when the roads are still clear. They should know I'll be there soon.

I stick my phone back into my pocket and continue to follow the pickup truck's tire tracks. The weeds aren't as high here, so I'll be able to avoid extra moisture soaking into my socks and jeans. I look up at the sky again and the rain hits me in the face. I'm not sure how many more hours of daylight I have left. This ominous thought makes my legs move faster.

As the cold air begins to seep through my clothing, my mind starts entertaining thoughts that I originally ignored when I started following this guy: What if Charity is telling the truth and her ex is after her? What if he is dangerous? But the answers to these questions are impossible to find out, unless I talk to him.

Maybe it's desperation that's making me do this. Maybe it's my love for Roy. All I know is that I'm in danger of losing him, and to me, that's scarier than confronting Charity's ex.

The only chance I have at staying together with Roy is almost within my grasp. I'll talk to Charity's ex, find out the truth about her past, then I'll prove to Roy that she's the one who can't be trusted.

Once she's out of the way and no longer interfering in Roy's life, all I will have to do is keep what happened between me and Spike a secret. And if Roy ever does find out what happened, I'll point the finger right back at him. After all, he cheated on me too.

CHAPTER 29

CHARITY (BELLANY)

The flood has blocked off access to the road that leads up the mountain, so the influx of hotel guests has officially ended. Spike and Tracy made it back in time. Samantha, on the other hand, wasn't so lucky. She's still missing. Cry me a river. Like I care.

All the rest of the hotel guests are tucked inside their rooms, nice and snug, fireplaces burning, TVs on, microwaves heating up stinky food. People are making trips to the vending machines, complaining about losing their money and their candy bars and bags of Skittles getting stuck.

I cleaned out the nasty refrigerator in the break room, and it's still packed full of food, all of Veronica's favorites: ice cream, pizza, bologna, hot dogs, cheesecake... The storage room has enough food stocked to feed the entire hotel for months. I helped myself to some of Veronica's food supply and brought it out here with me to the cottage.

This place is small, but it isn't that bad. It has internet access, a kitchenette, table and chairs, a TV, a couch, a queen-size bed, a rocking chair, and a fireplace. It could use some redecorating, but I actually like it better than the hotel. It's way more private out here.

When I open up the refrigerator, I discover that it's not working. Great. My sodas aren't chilling. Speaking of chilling, it's cold in here. I rub my hands together as I check the thermostat. The heat is on, so why isn't any hot air coming out of the vents? I'm going to freeze if I don't get a fire going. I open the cupboard attached to the fireplace, expecting to find wood, but it's empty. I put my gloves and coat on, then head outside to scavenge around for something I can burn, determined not to freeze tonight.

As I'm wandering around through the trees, my thoughts turn to my plans for Veronica and making sure I haven't overlooked something. Then I remember the Benadryl I saw in the storage room at the hotel. It's crucial I get some, otherwise this plan won't work.

When I return to the cottage, my arms full of firewood, I find the door cracked open. I could've sworn that I locked it.

I set down the pile of wood and cautiously step through the doorway. My bags and suitcase have been tossed. My clothes are everywhere. The window has been broken, which is how they got in here. But I wonder if they're still here.

This place is tiny, which is a good thing for situations such as this. I can see just about every inch of this place right from where I'm standing. Could they be under the bed? I guess it's high enough to squeeze under there. In the closet? The door is shut, so it's possible. The only other place to hide is the bathroom, and I can't see in there from here.

My eyes scan the room for something to use as a weapon. My pocketknife is mixed in with my stuff, clear on the other side of the bed. There isn't much to choose from that I can grab right here. This place is pretty bare.

I pick up a bookend from off the shelf and hold it up at the ready as I slowly make my way across the room, floorboards squeaking underneath my feet. My heart rate picks up, and my fingers tighten around the bookend. I turn the knob on the closet door and slowly open it. Light penetrates the darkness, revealing a dusty collection of men's clothing on hangers. I jab the bookend through the clothes like it's a sword. Nobody's here.

I start toward the bathroom next. The door is already open, and when I'm close enough, I can see from the mirror's reflection the entire bathroom, except for behind the shower curtain. My hands are getting sweaty. I wipe them on my jeans and readjust my grip on the bookend. Whoever broke in here, I swear if they jump out at me, I'm going to kill 'em. I stand in front of the shower curtain, my heart hammering in my chest. Just yank it open quick, I tell myself. Another deep breath, and I swipe the curtain to the side, metal rings scraping across the shower rod. I let out a breath. It's empty.

I turn around and stare at the bed. Every scary movie I've seen with this exact same scenario flashes through my mind. I really wish

I had my knife. I set the bookend down, eyes remaining fixed on the bed. Get it over with, I tell myself. Just do it. On the count of three: one…two…three. I drop to my hands and knees, the side of my face hovering over the floor. A huge gasp escapes my throat. It's clear. I roll over onto my back and lay there until my heart rate finally slows back down.

When I get up, I grab my phone and send Roy a text: Come to the cottage. Hurry!

I'll play the role of damsel in distress, giving Roy the opportunity to come to my rescue.

I start typing out another text explaining what's going on, but this time when I hit send it doesn't go through. I tap the button again, and it still won't go. I swipe the screen to look at my settings and find that there's no cell signal. Some of the customers at the diner said this happened the last time it flooded. Whatever. I guess it doesn't matter. Roy should get that first text I sent. He'll come. I know he will.

Instead of picking up my clothes, I leave everything as it is. Roy needs to see this mess. I start sifting through the piles of my belongings, checking to see if anything is missing.

No! No! I can't believe it! My laptop is gone!

If someone hacks my password, they'll discover my fake email accounts, along with the pictures I created and sent to Samantha and Roy. At least I've already cleared my browsing history. But the one thing I still have on there is that stupid podcast. I've been listening to Cam Whitmeyer. He's absolutely obsessed with me and has an entire podcast series dedicated to my story.

In the last episode I listened to, he interviewed the brother of Constance Perry, the girl who died when I hit her with Quentin's car. Her brother actually threatened to hunt me down and kill me. I'd like to see him try. He won't be able to find me. And his stupid sister shouldn't have been walking along the road in the dark. It's her fault I hit her. She ruined my life.

I'm so freaking mad. I want to know who broke in here. Either somebody's looking for dirt on me, or they want to sell my laptop and make some money. It could be any one of the hotel guests. Did Samantha do this? Is she here somewhere? Or maybe Tracy and Spike did it.

Then it dawns on me that maybe someone else is to blame. Could Veronica have taken my laptop? Nah. She would just use her key, she wouldn't break the window... Unless she didn't want me to suspect her. I shake my head. No. No way. She's too fat and out of shape to walk all the way out here. It couldn't have been her.

CHAPTER 30

ROY

I go to Samantha's room. The door is cracked open, but she's not here. Why would she leave her door open like this? There's no sign of a struggle. Her bags are all neatly piled on the bed. Among them a black polymer case with a distinctive pistol shape catches my eye.

I open the case and find a gun inside, already loaded, so I take it. Anyone could have come in here and stolen it. Plus I know from experience how dangerous guns can be.

My phone buzzes with a text from Charity. Come to the cottage. Hurry!

I try to text her back but it won't send. Something feels very wrong, so I stuff the gun in my waistband and take off running.

I find Charity on the front porch, sitting in the rocking chair, but she's not rocking. Her piercing green eyes are trained on me, reminiscent of a cat who's either ready to pounce on a mouse or waiting to be let outside. I'm not sure which one of these scenarios fits, not until I see a tear roll down her cheek. Neither of them do.

Somehow, I already knew this day would go terribly wrong, like the last time it flooded. My eyes dart around, looking for clues as to what might be upsetting her. That's when I notice the smashed window and the shattered glass scattered across the floor.

My mind races, filling in the gaps of missing information, anticipating the situation. I don't see any blood or bruising on Charity. Besides the tears, there's no other visible signs of distress. Her beautiful face, luscious pink lips, large eyes—that innocent yet alluring look she has, it's all still there—breathtaking like always. I wrinkle my eyes shut for a beat, chastising myself for letting my thoughts go there. She's in distress. Something's wrong. This isn't the time to fall under her spell.

Charity wipes her cheek with the bottom of her sleeve. She wouldn't be crying if she had broken the window because she accidentally got locked out. No. This is more serious than that. So who broke it?

Charity stands as I get closer. "It was already broken when I got here." She gestures to the window.

She walks toward the door, but hesitates as she passes me. Should I hug her? Is that what she wants? I keep my arms at my side for too long. The moment is gone.

She opens the door, and I can see her bag is lying open on the floor. Her clothes are strewn all over. As I survey the room, I see three more duffel bags have been dumped out onto the floor near the bathroom.

"I don't know who would do this? Or why?" My mind is shuffling through all of the different faces I've seen today and all of the interactions I've had with the hotel guests. Then my stomach tenses. Wait. There was someone who stood out from the rest of the guests. The guy who dressed like a cowboy. He was friendly, talkative, casual in his demeanor. I didn't think anything of it at the time, but now I'm realizing there might be more going on with him. He said he had met Charity at Jesse's Diner and that she recommended staying at Grandma's hotel. What did he say his name was? CJ? He was tall and had blond hair. Didn't Charity tell me that her ex was tall and blond? I think she did. Could CJ be her ex? Did he finally track her down?

Or maybe the guy in the blue pickup truck did this. He had blond hair. Maybe he's her ex. I'm not going to mention either of them though, not yet. She doesn't need a reminder to be careful. That's all she's been doing since she arrived here in Washington.

I look out the window at the dark sky settling into the trees. Grandma owns a seventy-five-acre parcel. Most of it is high enough to be safe from the flood. But we're also stuck up here, at least until the water recedes. And that could take days, maybe weeks.

This cottage is tucked back in the woods and hidden from the hotel guests. There's no way I would be able to hear Charity if she screamed or called for help. The cell phone signal just went down too. I have got to convince her to come back to the house with me.

I wouldn't feel comfortable leaving her out here alone. If something bad were to happen, I'd never forgive myself. "How about we gather up your stuff and head back to the house?"

Charity nods in agreement, and I think she's relieved to hear me suggest this.

After we collect all her things, she takes one last look around to make sure she hasn't forgotten anything. Then she starts to make the bed, but I insist that she just leave it. I pick up her suitcase, which looks ancient, probably a thrift store find made in the eighties. There aren't any wheels on it. I tuck it under my arm like a football, a rather large and heavy football, and watch her as she stands there deep in thought. I hope she isn't planning on trying to clean something else right now.

I pick up a duffel bag next, ready to leave. Luckily this one isn't that heavy. "Did you notice if anything was missing from your bags?" I ask. Did CJ or that other guy do this just to scare her? What else are they planning on doing?

"I'm not sure if anything's missing. I'll have to go through my stuff back at the house to double check." She picks up her phone and purse, then flicks off the light switch as we walk outside.

My arms are full, but I manage to balance everything as I pull the door shut behind us.

She holds out her hand, waiting. I give her a questioning look, unsure what she wants. I didn't bring a flashlight.

"I can carry another bag," she says.

"No. I got it." At least I think I do. But I'm already dreading the hike back to the house. The path isn't flat. It's bumpy, rocky, hilly, and full of exposed roots perfect for tripping over. I hope I don't fall like an idiot.

Charity walks slightly ahead of me, the light from her phone trained on the path. She glances over her shoulder. "I thought I'd be safe back here behind the house, you know? Far away from the hotel and all those frantic people trying to escape the flood." There's a shudder in her voice. She sounds nervous, maybe even scared.

"Sometimes people can get a little out of hand during a natural disaster." I make this general statement, because I don't want to bring up her ex-boyfriend.

She glances back again and stumbles but manages not to fall.

"Be careful," I say.

The duffel bag has slipped off her shoulder. She tugs it back up and continues walking. "The ground is kind of slippery."

We're surrounded by water up here on this mountain. The only way to get off it is to swim, but the water is freezing. Hypothermia would set in quickly. And the water's current is strong. It could carry away a person in an instant. I've seen it happen before. It's a memory I wish I could forget. If her ex is up here, he's not leaving. He's going to be here with us the entire time.

Charity slows down a bit, and I match her pace. We're walking alongside each other now since the path is wider here.

"Are you sure there's still room in the house for me?" she asks.

"Yeah. Of course there's still room."

"Thank you. For helping me."

"Sure." She doesn't need to thank me. I want to help her.

Twigs and leaves crunch beneath our feet. The air is still, the sky completely black. A couple drops of rain begin to fall on my face. Charity flips her hood up, shoulders hunched forward, trying to keep dry.

We're moving down the path more quickly now. Sporadic tree branches brush along my shoulders. It almost feels like someone's fingers are reaching out and touching me sometimes. Raindrops start coming faster, landing on the leaves, pelting the rocks. A loud snap of a twig gets my instant attention. The noise came from somewhere behind me. Charity stops and turns.

I reach my hand behind my back and feel the rough grip of the gun protruding from my waistband. It has been five years since the last time I shot a gun. But that's a memory I would rather not think about, so I push it out of my mind. I'm more concerned about Charity's ex. He already tried to kill her once.

Charity shifts the beam of her light, aiming it in the direction of the noise. My eyes strain to see clearly in the dark. The shapes and shadows all seem to mix together.

"Do you think it was just an animal?" she whispers.

"Yeah, probably," I reply, even though I'm really not sure. I just don't want to worry her.

"What's that?" she asks, her voice pitched slightly higher. She's staring at my hand poised behind my back. "Is that a gun?"

I don't know if she's frightened or relieved that I have this. But I need it. That guy in the pickup truck had a gun. If he's out here right now, I'm sure he has it with him.

The rain picks up, coming down much harder. Another snap of a twig sends my heart racing. Someone's out there. I see branches move in the dim light. I drop the bags and pull out the gun.

Charity's pressed up against my back. "I think I saw someone," she whispers. The noise comes again, this time closer, louder. My stomach knots up. I lift the gun and my finger curls around the trigger.

CHAPTER 31

ROY

I'm staring into the darkness as the gunshot echoes in my ears. The rain is still falling, only I can't hear it anymore. What was I thinking? How could I have been so careless? I didn't mean to actually pull the trigger. I barely touched it. The last time I shot a gun, I was aiming at a target. This time I shot blindly, straight into the dark, by accident.

Charity's cold fingers cover my hand, gently directing me to lower the gun.

The echoing finally stops and the sound of the rain returns. She's standing next to me. Is she breathing heavily, or is it me? Am I the one out of breath? My heart feels like it's going to explode in my chest.

"Do you hear anything?" I ask her, as the rain pelts my face. For a second, maybe two, I think I hear crying. No. It can't be. Those are the cries from my nightmares, when I relive what happened the last time I shot a gun. It wasn't dark that day. It was broad daylight. I could see everything perfectly.

Charity aims the light from her phone directly into the trees. She wraps her arm around mine, her body pressed in close. "We should probably go check to see if you hit anyone."

CHAPTER 32

ROY

When Grandma sees me and Charity soaking wet, dripping all over the floor, she sets down her bag of Doritos and mutes the TV. "What happened to you two? Did you fall into the floodwater?"

It would be easier to just say yes than to tell Grandma how we have been wandering around in the dark and the freezing rain, with a possible stalker on the loose, and what happened with the gun. I'm not telling her any of that. "It's just from the rain," I reply and head up the stairs with Charity. Roscoe follows us, but only makes it up two steps before he turns back around.

"Is there a problem with the cottage?" Grandma asks, eyeing Charity.

"She needs to stay here tonight."

Grandma grunts and I know she's not pleased. She reaches back into her Doritos bag. "If that rain doesn't stop, we're all gonna be stuck up here...maybe for weeks."

I turn to Charity and shake my head. "She's just exaggerating," I say in a low voice.

I show Charity to her room, set down her bags, and point out the adjoining bathroom. "There should be towels, shampoo, soap, and everything else you need in there."

She smiles at me as if this is just a normal night, like nothing happened—like I never fired the gun, the cottage was never broken into, and the flood isn't even happening. She's walking around the room commenting on how nice it is.

I'm relieved she's not upset with me, but I'm still mad at myself. That was really stupid what I did. I should know better. What kind of a coward gets scared and just starts firing his gun at a random noise?

I step into the doorway, about to leave. "Help yourself to anything in the house: food, the laundry room, the TV, whatever."

Charity stares at me in a way that makes me wonder if I'm forgetting something. "Is there anything else you need?"

She smiles, then sighs before turning to open up her suitcase. "Looks like I still have some dry clothes. I should be fine."

"I'm heading back over to the hotel to check on some stuff." What I'm not telling her is that I'm also going back out into the woods. I'm not convinced that I didn't shoot someone.

Charity stops looking through her suitcase. "Want me to come?"

She is soaking wet, and I don't want her to get sick. She needs to warm herself up. "You should probably stay here. I've got some things I need to do."

She tosses some clothes onto the bed. "Maybe we can play a game of poker when you get back?"

"Maybe." I wipe my hand across my forehead to dry my face, then start heading down the stairs. Something has been nagging at me. I finally realize what it is and my chest constricts. I had been so focused on the possibility that it was Charity's ex out in the woods that I hadn't even considered the other possibility. Samantha. She has been missing for hours. What if it was her out there, following us, and I just shot her?

I race down the stairs and hear Grandma call after me, but I keep going, fearing the worst has happened.

CHAPTER 33

SPIKE

I hear pounding and run to see if it's Samantha. As soon as I enter the hallway, my hope is once again dashed to pieces. It's Roy and he's drenched. He turns to look at me, pointing at the door to Samantha's room. "Is she in here?"

What a jerk. Is this the first time he's come to check? My eyes start to narrow but searing pain stops me. My fist clenches, and I want so badly to deck him right now for giving me a black eye.

"Is she in here?" he asks again, raising his voice.

"Why don't you have a look for yourself?"

I'm on his heels as he enters her room. I haven't been able to come in here since Tracy gave him back the key. I've kept our hotel room door cracked open to listen for her. So far, I haven't heard anything, but I'm still hoping that maybe she's here and I just missed her somehow.

Roy heads to the bathroom while I check the closet. Empty. She hasn't come back, not since she dropped off her stuff. Her bags are still zipped up, packed full of all her things, and the bed is still made.

Roy starts grilling me, wanting to know if Tracy and I have any new information. "Has she called? Texted?"

I've been trying all night and haven't gotten through. "No," I snap. "We have no idea where she is."

"Is Tracy still up?"

"She's asleep, and don't go in there to wake her up. She needs to get some rest. She's been worried sick about Samantha."

"Have you been able to get in touch with her dad?"

I chuckle. "Why would he know where she is? That guy's probably passed out drunk in some casino hotel room. He doesn't care about Samantha." Roy doesn't argue with my logic. I'm sure he knows I'm right. "Were you finally out looking for her? Is that why you're all wet?"

Roy looks at me but doesn't answer.

"For Samantha's sake, I hope you were out looking for her. Because if she finds out that you were sitting on your butt at the hotel while she was out there stranded—"

"Shut up! I was outside looking for her."

I highly doubt that. "So where did you go?"

"I've been looking around the property, through the woods, up and down the trails."

He still should have gone with me earlier instead of staying here. Stuck-up rich boy, thinks he's better than me because he has money. "Just go, man. She ain't here."

"If you hear from her—"

"I know, I know. I'm sure Tracy will be courteous enough to let you know that she's back." Because I'm sure not gonna do it.

He pulls a flashlight from his pocket. "I'm heading back outside to look for her."

"Sure you are." This guy is such a joke.

Roy points at me with his flashlight, face all contorted with anger. "I was going to ask if you wanted to come."

Oh, I see. Now he's trying to guilt-trip me. I don't think so, buddy. I'm not going to let him one-up *me*. "Let me get my coat."

CHAPTER 34

CHARITY (BELLANY)

Little Roscoe is out cold, thanks to the help of Benadryl. I found some in Veronica's medicine cabinet. I slid him under her bed, completely out of sight, and I know she won't look for him there. Bending over is not something Veronica does. Ever.

She's been running all over the house looking for him. Well… her version of running, calling his name, getting out of breath. I run around the house looking for him too, as if I care about the ugly mutt.

Veronica is all too eager to go look for him outside once I point out that the door has been left open. I am the one who opened it. She's blaming Roy, just like I knew she would.

I borrow one of Veronica's raincoats and a pair of her rain boots, which are both way too big. I'm still freezing, but at least I'm not as wet as I was before.

We've been wandering around out here for at least an hour now. I wish she would stop yelling out Roscoe's name. I don't want Roy to hear her. I left him a note back at the house, per Veronica's insistence. When he gets back and reads it, I know he'll come looking for us. He could show up any moment.

I continue to steer Veronica down the hill, away from her house. *Don't run out of steam on me now, old woman, keep that love for Roscoe burning inside and pushing that fat body of yours along.*

Veronica slips and nearly falls. *Careful, Ol' Bessy, don't hurt yourself, not yet anyway.*

"That was close," she says, slightly out of breath.

I don't want to suggest this, but I feel like I should keep up the charade, for appearances' sake. "Maybe we should head back to the house."

She wipes the rain from her face, the worried look even more pronounced. I think she's afraid I want to give up. She bites her lip. Is she trying to make me feel guilty for wanting to go back? What a manipulator.

"I don't know what I'll do if we don't find him," she says.

"Don't worry," I assure her. "We'll find him."

She wipes her face again, peering out at the trees and the black sky. "He used to stay close to me. He's a good dog, really. I should have just hired someone to train him better…"

Would have, should have, could have. Blah, blah, blah. I don't want to listen to this. Let's keep moving.

Veronica points her flashlight in the exact direction I want to go, and I almost smile. This is turning out to be easier than I thought.

CHAPTER 35

SPIKE

I'm not familiar with the trails that run through these woods. Roy is leading, and I'm following, which is ticking me off. He already thinks he's better than me. But he's no mountain man, expert tracker. He's a pretty boy who sits around all day answering phones like a secretary.

Roy stops suddenly, and I almost run into him. "Did you hear that? I thought I heard someone yelling."

I didn't hear anything. This guy must be losing his mind. "Yelling? What were they saying?" Maybe he's just hearing the voices inside his own head. I wipe the rain from my one good eye. "Are we going to keep searching? Or are we gonna stand here?"

"Shh!"

"Don't shush me!"

"I heard something. Be quiet."

Okay, loser. Go ahead, keep up with your nonsense.

I have no idea what Samantha sees in this guy. It's gotta be the money. Well, I'm going to make my own money someday, and I'm not going to have it handed to me by some rich relative. I'm going to work hard and make my own way in the world. I'll be rich and successful, no doubt about it. I've got plenty of plans, lots of ideas. I'll open up my own garage, hire top-notch mechanics. I'll have the best shop in town. We'll do custom, top-of-the-line work. Then I'll expand to the neighboring cities. I'll eventually sell my franchise and make loads of money. Samantha and I will travel the world vacationing. I'll buy her a fancy engagement ring—

"Over there!" Roy shouts, interrupting my thoughts.

"Over there, what?" Again, I still don't hear anything.

"Let's go this way."

I think he's making this up, but whatever. I'll go ahead and follow him. It's not like I'm going to be able to find my way back to the hotel without getting lost a few times. If Samantha is out here, which I highly doubt, the last thing I want is for Roy to find her without me.

He makes a right turn, leaving the trail, and I'm right on his heels as we weave through the trees.

Samantha's probably stuck in her car somewhere. I'm sure she'll stay there to try and keep warm and avoid getting drenched by the rain. She wouldn't be wandering around out here in the black of night. She's not that stupid. I'm sure she would wait until daylight to hike back to the hotel. But I'm not going to say this to Roy. He'll think I'm giving up or that I'm chickening out. I'll keep going as long as he does. I can keep up.

CHAPTER 36

CHARITY (BELLANY)

When I get back to the house, I run right upstairs to check on Roscoe. I'm not sure if I gave him too much Benadryl. I hope I didn't kill him.

I push up the bed's dust ruffle and grab ahold of him. He doesn't wake up, but he is still breathing. I pick him up, take him to the laundry room, and set him inside one of the baskets on a bunch of dirty clothes. I'm about to leave, but decide I should cover him up with some of the clothes, at least a bit. Roscoe needs to be hidden. If he's easy to find, then it wouldn't make sense for Veronica and I to go out in the woods looking for him.

I start down the hallway, feeling frustrated. My plan to push Veronica into the floodwater failed. We were right there, so close. If she wasn't such a heifer, I would have dragged her into the water, but she never quite got close enough to guarantee success. Even with the slippery mud, I doubt I'd be able to slide her in there. She kept insisting that I come back to the hotel to find Roy so that he could help us look for Roscoe. I tried to change her mind, but she wouldn't listen to me. So Veronica's still out there wandering around with her flashlight looking for a dog that isn't lost.

My fingers are numb. My pants and socks are soaked. These boots are crap and don't keep the rainwater out. As soon as I find Roy, I need another hot shower and to come up with a new plan. This has been a total waste of time.

I reach in my pocket for my phone so I can text him, forgetting that the cell signal is down. I climb in bed and try to warm up. Where are you, Roy? If he's snuggled up with Samantha in her room right now, I swear I'm gonna lose it.

I startle awake, eyes popping open, at the sound of the house door slamming. I must have fallen asleep. I quickly stand up and run my fingers through my hair as footsteps echo through the house.

"Who's there?" I call, rushing downstairs to check.

Roy and Spike appear, and they're both soaking wet. Wow. Spike's eye is black and blue and swollen shut. I scan Roy's face. It doesn't look like Spike retaliated in any way.

Time for me to act worried. "Where have you been?" I say.

Roy sets his flashlight down on the kitchen counter. "I've been hiking through the woods looking for Samantha."

"You mean *we've* been looking for Samantha," Spike corrects.

I feel uneasy about talking to Roy, since I have no idea where

Veronica is or if she came back. Then I hear Roscoe bark. He comes running into the kitchen, his tail wagging.

"Roscoe!" I gasp. "Where have you been?" I scoop him up into my arms and snuggle him close. "Veronica and I were outside looking for him, but here he is, safe and sound. I came back to find you, and I guess I collapsed with exhaustion until I heard you come in." I continue to explain to Roy that I'm not sure if Veronica is still outside or if she's back.

He checks her room, calling out for her, but she doesn't answer. Then he swipes the flashlight off the counter, rushing out the back door. I'm racing to get my boots and coat on and follow after him.

Spike's right behind us. "Slow down."

Roy spins around. "Make sure that door is shut."

"I know, I know." Spike pulls the door closed behind him. "Wouldn't want the runt to get out again," he says in a low voice so Roy can't hear. But I heard him.

Roy's calling out for Veronica.

Spike joins in, "Veronica!"

I follow along, shouting for her too.

There's definite panic in Roy's voice. I'm afraid he's going to turn on me and blame me for all of this. It's of critical importance that he understands that I'm just as concerned as he is.

We eventually get to the bottom of the hill. I point my flashlight. "Roy. We should go this way. That's where Veronica was looking before."

"Thank you," he says.

I let out a breath, full of relief. At least I don't think he's mad at me.

Spike is grumbling and complaining about something, but I can't make out what he's saying. Miraculously, Roy is ignoring him and hasn't managed to punch him in the other eye yet.

Spike starts calling Samantha's name, instead of Veronica's. Roy doesn't follow suit. He's only calling for Veronica.

Roy is moving so fast, I'm having a hard time keeping up. I'm concerned that if we find Veronica out here lying on the ground, dead from a heart attack, that Roy will freak out and blame me for what happened, even though it's not my fault—well, I mean it *is* my fault, but he doesn't know that.

Spike's grumbling is getting louder. I can finally hear what he's saying. "She gets herself lost and all for a dumb dog."

He's speaking the truth. It was stupid of Veronica to place herself in danger for Roscoe. That right there is her own fault.

We finally arrive at the place where I originally left Veronica, near the steep drop-off that leads directly into the floodwaters. I shine the beam of my flashlight at what used to be a tiny creek. Now it's a raging river. I think the water level has risen even more since last time I was here.

What a twist of fate it would be if she ended up falling into the water all on her own without any extra help from me.

The rain continues to land on my face, collecting on my eyelashes. I blink it away and imagine my new future. I'm so close to having everything I want: money, stability, power, and of course Roy. Suddenly I'm not feeling as cold anymore, and the rain isn't bothering me either.

"Over here!" Spike yells.

My stomach flips. Please don't let her be alive.

Roy and I rush over to him, the beams of our flashlights converging on the exact same spot. My eyes dart around, searching, but I don't see her. Spike has only found Veronica's flashlight. It's sitting on the ground close to the water's edge.

I step forward and bend down to pick it up. My breath catches. The muddy ground under my boots gives way, and I can't stop myself from sliding toward the rushing water. A scream escapes my throat. It's as if everything is happening in slow motion, and I'm powerless to stop it. Visions of my hopes and dreams are crumbling down all around me. Is this how it all ends? My hands flail around, searching for something to grab onto. The sting of the ice-cold water works its way up my legs, my waist, my chest. I can't breathe!

CHAPTER 37

SPIKE

One second Charity's standing right beside me, and the next she's falling into the water. I can't believe how fast Roy reacts. He snatches hold of Charity's wrist and lets out a loud Chewbacca groan as he pulls her from the water. He tumbles onto his back.

Charity's crying, still clinging to Roy like he's a life jacket and she's a passenger on the *Titanic*.

"It's okay," he says, holding her against his chest. "I got you. You're all right. You're safe."

I'm standing here still stunned at what just happened. "Man, Roy, you must have a guardian angel watching over you, because that ground is muddy and slippery. Look at it. How did you get her back up here without falling in?" I chuckle. "You're a freaking lucky dog, you know that?" I hold out my trembling hand. "Look at me. I'm shaking. Man, Charity, I thought you were a goner."

Charity is still clinging onto Roy. Even though it's dark out here, I would have to be blind not to see how in love this girl is with him. Shoot. He just saved her life and that's like a swift ticket to the front of the line. She wants him bad.

Roy helps Charity stand up, keeping his arm around her. I don't know where their flashlights went, probably in the water. But I've still got mine. I pick up the extra one we found on the ground and pass it over to Roy. When he takes it from me, he stares at it for a couple beats.

I know what he's thinking, because I'm thinking the same thing too. What if his grandma wasn't as lucky as Charity? That flood-water probably swallowed her up. She's gone forever. Who knows, maybe her body will get washed out to sea. That's what happened to a little boy the last time it flooded. He was up here on this same mountain. I remember how freaked out everyone was when they heard he was missing.

Charity is shivering hard. She got completely soaked. As cold as it is tonight, she's going to be in trouble if she stays in those wet clothes much longer.

"Dude, we need to get her back to the house. Look at her, she's shivering. She's probably got hypothermia."

Roy turns and looks at the surging river again, then up the bank before pivoting to face me.

I could offer to take Charity back to the house, but I doubt she wants to go anywhere without Roy. "I'm cold too," I tell him. "Come on, man. We can come back out and search later."

Roy hesitates again until Charity goes limp in his arms, her head dropping to the side.

That can't be good.

He scoops her up without another word and sets off for the house.

CHAPTER 38

CHARITY (BELLANY)

I wake to a bright beam of daylight landing on my face. It must have stopped raining. I sit up on the couch, wondering where Roy is. The last thing I remember was sitting here with him, wrapped up in his arms and a couple of blankets.

I'm no longer shivering, but last night I thought I would never warm up. The unrelenting sting of cold that I felt was like tiny needles stabbing my entire body. The traumatic memory is still fresh in my mind, partly because I can't believe it actually happened and partly because I can't believe how close I came to dying.

Spike's sitting on the couch near my feet, slumped over and snoring. Roscoe's asleep on his lap.

I nudge his arm with my foot. "Hey." No response. I nudge him again, harder, and he finally opens his eyes. "Wake up. Where's Roy?"

Spike stretches his arms overhead, yawning, like this is just another typical morning and he doesn't have a care in the world. One more yawn before he sits forward, finally ready to turn on that dense brain of his and speak. "I think he went outside to go look for Veronica again." Spike shakes his head, making a face. "I told him just to accept the inevitable. She's either been swept up in the flood or she's lying out there dead from exposure to the cold. There's no sense in hoping for a better outcome."

I would definitely lay odds on Veronica being dead. Killing her was my original plan, but I didn't do it. Sure, I drugged Roscoe and hid him so she'd go looking for him, and I kept leading her toward the rising floodwater, but I didn't push her in. I wasn't there when she fell. I'm sure that's what happened to her. The reason I slipped into the water was because I was standing on the exact same spot she was. She had already left a muddy path nice and slick for my feet to follow.

The woman was ancient and not in good health, getting meaner by the day. Her husband wasn't around anymore. The only reason for her to keep living was to be here for Roy. But he doesn't need her. I'm going to take care of him now.

Spike grabs his phone, like he's just remembering something important. "I wonder if Samantha called." His fingers skate across the screen, then he frowns. "Still no cell service." He stuffs his feet into his shoes. "I'm gonna go back to the hotel and see if she's there."

"I hope she is," I say, as if I care.

I get up from the couch and head to my bedroom. After I shower and do my makeup, I plan on walking over to the hotel too. With Veronica gone, and Roy still searching for her, there is nobody left to take care of the guests. It's basically my hotel now anyway. I should look after my investment. I'm sure Roy will be busy all day wandering around the endless acres of property searching in vain for Veronica, and Samantha.

As soon as I finish blow-drying my hair, I hear a knock on my bedroom door. "Charity?" Spike calls from the other side.

"One second." I pull on a pair of jeans and a T-shirt, conceal my switchblade in a pocket, then open the door.

Spike comes in and watches me put my socks on. He's not saying anything, so I prompt him to get that brain of his working again. "What do you want?"

"Tracy and I are about to head out again and look for Samantha. We're going to hike the trail down to the campground. Maybe we'll run into Roy out there. Do you want to come?"

No, bozo. Somebody's got to stay at the hotel. "I'm going to cover the hotel office duties." I grab one of my shoes and loosen the laces. "I'm sure the hotel guests are lined up waiting for someone to help them."

"My dad said he could cover the office, if you wanted him to. Then you can come with us to look for Roy and Samantha."

I grab my other shoe, trying to decide what to do. I don't think taking care of the hotel ranks up there as being most important to Roy right now. He's probably emotionally devastated; he has already lost his mother, his grandfather, and now his grandmother. He doesn't have anyone else left. Except for me. I need to be there for him.

"That sounds like a great idea," I say, standing in front of the mirror and picking up my hairbrush. "I'll open up the office and show your dad around real quick, then we can go."

Spike nods in agreement. "But first, I've gotta get something to eat."

I pull on a sweater, adding another layer of clothing to help me stay warm. It's also important that I look good for Roy. I quickly apply some waterproof eye makeup and braid my hair. All I need now is a baseball cap. That would finish off my look nicely.

I head to Roy's bedroom and survey his vast collection of baseball caps. My attention is drawn to a camouflage one with a fishhook sticking out of it. For a moment, my thoughts are invaded with a memory of Quentin. He had a camouflage baseball cap similar to this one. Sometimes I really miss him…and the life I thought we would have together.

I pick out a plain black baseball cap instead, put it on, and walk over to the mirror. This looks perfect. As I turn to head out of Roy's bedroom, I notice a basketball on the floor next to his bed. For a split second, a haunting image flashes in my mind—Quentin's motionless body lying on the floor and the brick in my hand. I push the memory away, but I am hit with a realization: Basketball and baseball caps aren't the only similarities between Roy and Quentin. I'm picking a *type*. I feel like this deserves some deep self-analysis, but I don't have time for that sort of thing right now.

"You ready?" Spike calls, pulling me from my thoughts. He's standing there chomping on a half-eaten bagel. "You should get something to eat. We could be gone all day." He pats his jacket pocket. "I've got some extra stuff for later too."

"Yeah, I'll get something," I say, grabbing my coat.

CHAPTER 39

CHARITY (BELLANY)

Standing outside the door, I find Mr. and Mrs. Sims, the lovely couple who are blackmailing Veronica. I wonder if they got her note informing them that she's not going to pay the extra three hundred dollars a month. Is that what they're here to talk about? Well, little do they know, their cash cow has just keeled over; too bad for them, but they're not going to be getting any more money.

I smile as if it's business as usual, unlock the door, and invite them inside.

"Charity?" Mr. Sims gives me a strange look. "I thought you worked at the diner."

"I do. And I help out here too. This is my second job." *Any more questions, Sherlock?*

Mrs. Sims places a five-dollar bill on the counter, and I give her a questioning look. "The vending machine won't take it," she explains. "It keeps spitting it back out. Those machines are old and don't work right. We tried every single one and had the exact same result."

They want money for the vending machines? Are they going to be this annoying the entire time they stay here? Didn't they bring any other food with them?

I pick up the bill and want to roll my eyes. It's wrinkled and torn in the corner, but of course it's the machine's fault. "How about if I give you quarters?" I open up the cash drawer and count out the money.

"Anything else?" I ask politely.

Mr. Sims makes a face. "Is there any chance we could stay in a different room? Our bed is lumpy. We didn't get much sleep last night."

There is nothing wrong with their bed. "Sorry. We're completely booked."

Mrs. Sims brushes a strand of greasy hair out of her face, leaning in close as if she's going to tell me a secret. "Charity. You should find someplace else to work. Veronica is an evil, evil woman."

Whoa. Now we're getting somewhere. Hit me with the gossip. I'm all ears. "Mrs. Sims, why would you say such a thing?"

Mr. Sims places his hand on her shoulder. "Darling," he says to her. "She'll be fine. I'm sure she can take care of herself. It's going to be okay."

"No, it's not okay." Mrs. Sims brushes his hand away. "I didn't want to come here. I hate this place! I hate that woman!" Tears begin filling her eyes. "She took my little boy from me."

Wait, what? "Veronica took your son from you?"

"She said she would give him back when I was able to take care of him. We didn't have any money. I was desperate—I didn't know what else to do."

"I don't understand."

Mrs. Sims starts shaking. "She forced me to sell my own child—"

"That's enough," Mr. Sims interrupts her. "Come on, you're not making any sense. You need to take your pills and get something to eat." He takes his wife by the shoulders to turn her around.

She pushes him away. "Don't touch me!"

Yeah, don't touch her. I want to hear the rest of this.

Mr. Sims shakes his head. "She needs to take her medicine. Whenever she doesn't take it, she starts talking nonsense."

"I know what I'm talking about!" Mrs. Sims shouts.

Again, Mr. Sims tries to physically steer her out of the lobby. She whirls around and smacks him in the face. The sound echoes. Mr. Sims stands there, stunned, then he storms off, slamming the door behind him.

I walk around to the other side of the counter, bringing with me a box of tissues and one of Veronica's bags of mini candy bars.

"Come on over here," I say, directing her to the couch. I sit down next to her and dangle the bag in front of her until she takes one. While I wait for her to finish eating it, she reaches into the bag a second time, her hand trembling. "I'm hypoglycemic..."

I nod, listening to her explain how low blood sugar affects her.

"Todd always tells me to take my pills, every time I want to talk about my boy."

"I'm so sorry."

"I take pills for my anxiety and depression. I'm not crazy." More tears fall.

"Of course you're not. You're just a grieving mother." I set the bag of chocolate to the side so she'll continue to talk and stop eating. I don't have much time to spare. Spike and Tracy will be here any minute with their dad. "What happened to your son?" I ask.

"She gave him to her daughter, Jessica."

My mouth literally drops open. Did I hear her correctly? Is she Roy's mother?

She blows her nose and wipes away a couple tears. "Jessica couldn't have children of her own." She blows her nose again. "I'm not supposed to talk about it. She paid me not to talk about it. If she finds out that I told you, she'll stop sending us money."

This isn't good. If Roy finds out, he'll insist on sharing his inheritance with them. He'll probably move them into Veronica's house. I'll be back to square one. It'll be years before any of this is mine. I can't let that happen.

I offer Mrs. Sims another tissue. "Is Mr. Sims Roy's biological father?"

"No. Roy's father died years ago of an aneurysm. When I gave my son up, I hadn't even met Todd yet."

The last thing I want is for her to find out that Veronica is dead. Then she'll have no incentive to keep her mouth shut, because she won't be getting any more money. She'll tell Roy everything. I've got to get rid of these two before the news about Veronica gets out. "Mrs. Sims."

She looks up at me with her reddened, tear-filled eyes. "My name is Pam."

"Pam," I say. "What if I could give you a lot of money—thousands of dollars to last you for years and years to come? Then you and your husband could move someplace else and get a fresh start. You can leave all of these painful memories behind."

The puzzled expression on her face doesn't surprise me. I kind of hit her with this all at once. But I had to. I'm on a time crunch here. The wrinkle between her eyebrows deepens. Her eyelashes blink rapidly. "But how would we get all that money? Veronica won't give it to us. My husband just recently asked her for more money and she refused to pay it." Pam pauses, her frown deepening. "We're behind on our rent, about to be evicted."

This couldn't be more perfect. She's desperate for money. "Don't worry about Veronica," I say as I lock the lobby door. I race around to the other side of the counter. "Pam, I'm going to write you a check for ten thousand dollars, and I'm going to sign Veronica's name. As soon as the floodwaters recede, take this to the bank and cash it. Then you and your husband need to leave town immediately, before Veronica finds out. Here's my email address," I say, writing it on a sticky note. "I want you to email me your bank account information. Then I'll transfer ten grand into your account every month, for the next ten months."

She still has a confused look on her face.

"That's one hundred thousand dollars, Pam."

Her brows shoot up. "What if we get caught? What if Veronica finds out?"

I begin filling in the numbers on the check. "You won't get caught if you are quick to get out of town. Go someplace far away, where Veronica can't find you."

She stares at the sticky note, reading my email address. "But why would you do this? You could get in as much trouble as us. What if you get caught and can't transfer all the money?"

"I'll tell you exactly why I'm doing this," I say, as if I'm some kind of modern-day Robin Hood, taking money from the rich to give to the poor. "I'm doing this because it's the right thing to do. Veronica took Roy from you. She deserves to have this money taken from her."

"Yeah... She does deserve it."

I place my hand on hers, in hopes of calming her fears. "As long as I keep the amount at ten thousand dollars a month, I don't think Veronica will notice the money is missing. She has several bank accounts. I'll be taking the money from an account she hardly ever checks."

The crease between Pam's eyebrows appears again. "But what happens when she finds out? How will we get the rest of our money?"

I smile and give her hand a reassuring pat. "If Veronica finds out, then I'll take the cash from her safe, and I'll personally deliver it to you." Veronica doesn't own a safe, but Pam doesn't need to know that; just like she doesn't need to know that Veronica is already dead.

"What if you get caught before you can get us the rest of the money?"

If this woman doesn't shut up and stop questioning me, I think I'm gonna lose it. I clench my teeth together, trying to calm myself down. "I promise you, I will do whatever it takes to keep myself out of jail. If that means I have to go on the run too, then I will."

"But why would you risk so much for us—"

I smack my hand down on the counter, startling her. "Pam," I say sternly. "I didn't want to tell you this, but I guess I have to." I pause and take a calming, deep breath. "I have already stolen money from Veronica and kept it for myself. I'm already taking a risk."

Pam looks at me wide-eyed.

"Veronica has hurt people. She deserves to pay. You agree with me, right?"

"Well, yes," she says.

"And when someone has to pay, that means someone else needs to collect. Are you following me?"

She nods.

I place a hand over my heart. "But I'm not the only person Veronica has hurt. It's not fair for me to be the only person who collects…is it?"

"No, it's not," she says, shaking her head.

"It's simple. I help you, and you help me. We both make Veronica pay for what she's done. So now you know my secret, and you should be assured that I know what I'm doing here. Trust me, I'm not an idiot. You will get all of your money."

Pam stares at the check and begins to reach for it, but stops.

"We don't have a lot of time to discuss this, Pam. Veronica could walk in any minute. This is a one-time offer," I say, holding out the check. "Are you in or out?"

There's knocking on the door. We both turn and look. Great. It's Spike, Tracy, and their dad.

Pam snatches the check from my hand and whispers, "I'm in."

I lean forward, eyes wide and serious. "This will be our secret. Don't tell anyone, except for your husband. As soon as you cash this check, leave town. Just get in your car and go."

She sighs. "I don't know how I'll explain this to Todd. We don't have anywhere to go."

I grab hold of her arm. "I'm sure Todd wants you to be happy. You need to get away from Veronica and from Chehalis. He'll understand."

Pam nods in agreement.

"You should leave the state, and if I were you, I wouldn't ever, under any circumstances, come back here. Not twenty years from now. Not even after you hear Veronica has passed away from old age. That check is your ticket to get out of here. Forever."

My words have stunned her to silence. The wheels in her head are definitely spinning. I can see it in her eyes.

"Agreed?" I prompt her.

Pam gives me a half nod. "Okay. I'll make sure we leave as soon as we can."

I walk to the door with her, but before I unlock it I give her a hug. "I'm so sorry you've had to endure all these years of grief and sadness. Your life will be better now. I know it will."

She squeezes her arms around me tighter. "Thank you, dear."

As I reach for the latch on the door, she touches my arm to stop me. "One more thing."

Spike bangs his fist on the door shouting something, but his voice sounds muffled.

"What is it, Pam?" I say impatiently.

"There was a man wandering the halls last night looking for you."

"Are you certain he was looking for me?" I ask, hoping she's mistaken.

"He described what you look like. He knew your name."

That's weird. "So what did this man look like? Did he say what his name was?"

"His name is CJ, and he said he met you at Jesse's Diner." Pam reaches her hand up high in the air. "He was about this tall. He was thin and had blue eyes. He was wearing a cowboy hat. I think he likes you."

I force a smile even though I feel uneasy about this news. I don't remember meeting anyone named CJ at the diner. "Thanks for letting me know." I open the door.

"Bye, dear," she says as she walks past me.

"Bye."

Spike bursts into the lobby first. "It's about time. Why didn't you open the door for us? What were you talking to that lady about?"

"It was important hotel business," I say, defensively.

Tracy's giving me a dirty look, but she's not intimidating. She looks like a clown; red hair sticking up in every direction, mascara smeared under her eyes. "We need to get going," she snaps.

I turn my focus to their father and give him a quick rundown of where everything is in the office. Then Tracy, Spike, and I are on our way, heading toward one of the hiking trails.

My thoughts return to Pam again. I still can't believe she's Roy's biological mother. Veronica should have just told Roy the truth after Jessica died. But no, Veronica preferred to keep paying Pam every month to keep her dirty secret.

I suspect that Veronica was worried Roy might never forgive her if he found out the truth. After her daughter and husband passed away, he was all she had left. She couldn't risk losing him too.

I mull this over and conclude that's not the entire explanation. I observed Veronica enough to know that she was the kind of person who enjoyed being hated and feared. She needed a power trip like an addict needs their drugs. I suspect the monthly payments weren't just hush money to keep her victims quiet. She used them as a way to constantly remind Pam and Todd that she was still in control—still setting the terms.

I bet Todd is dancing around his hotel room right now, celebrating. He's probably imagining how he'll spend the money.

Pam missed her window of opportunity to be involved in Roy's life. She should never have agreed to sell her child to Veronica.

They will collect their money, move on, and probably become regulars at some other diner in some new town. But I bet they'll still be horrible tippers.

Roy is definitely better off without them.

CHAPTER 40

SAMANTHA

As soon as I wake up, I put my shoes and coat back on, then unzip the tent. The chill in the morning air gives me a shiver. Mack's probably still asleep in his trailer, so I'm not going to say goodbye to him. He let me stay in his tent when I told him I got stuck here last night. The water flooded the road before I could drive back to the hotel.

I know where the guy in the blue pickup truck is camping. I watched him from a distance last night, too afraid to actually talk to him. But I think I've built up enough courage to do it this morning. I spent all night thinking about what I'll say and how things might play out. I think I'm ready.

There's a small campfire burning next to his truck. He's got a tent set up, some clothes hanging on a line to dry. He's sitting on a camp chair with a mug in his hand. He seems harmless, really. He's just like most of these other people out here, stuck until the floodwater recedes.

When he sees me approach, he rises to his feet. He doesn't have any shoes on. His socks and shoes are drying by the fire. He smiles at me. "I don't have any coffee, but I do have hot chocolate. Do you want some?"

He's a friendly guy; seems nice. "Sure. Thank you."

"My name's Perry." He picks up a mug and starts pouring hot water into it.

"I'm Samantha."

"Nice to meet you, Samantha." He nods toward the camp chair. "Feel free to have a seat."

It looks like this might be his only chair. I sit down, and he hands me a hot chocolate. The heat of the mug feels good on my cold fingers.

He takes a sip from his mug.

"Where are you from?" I ask him.

He grins. "What makes you think I'm not from around here?"

"Are you from around here?"

He shakes his head. "No. I'm actually from Virginia." He takes a seat on a nearby tree stump.

If he is Charity's ex, then shouldn't he be from Texas? That's where she said she was from. "So what brought you here to Chehalis?" I ask.

He gives me another smile, like he's amused about something. "I'm kind of a wanderer. I like to travel around the country."

My stomach grumbles and Perry notices. "You're hungry." He passes me a box of Pop-Tarts. "Help yourself to as many as you want."

"Thanks." I take one, then hand the box back to him.

He opens up a pack and takes a bite. "These would be better if they were toasted," he says, looking at the fire.

"I always eat them like this."

He smiles again, and I'm feeling uncomfortable at how friendly he's being. Shouldn't I feel the opposite? This is what I wanted. I wanted him to talk to me so I could ask him questions. Maybe I'm afraid that Charity's stories about her ex are true. Maybe he is a dangerous guy.

Perry scans the other nearby campsites. "So where are you camped out at? Are you here by yourself?"

His questions seem harmless enough, and under any other circumstance I wouldn't read so much into them, but I feel like he's overstepping. He shouldn't be asking me if I'm alone. "I'm a guest of Mack, the guy who runs the campground." The guy you snuck past yesterday, instead of coming in through the main entrance. I take a bite of my Pop-Tart, trying to read his facial expression, but he doesn't seem to react any differently.

I'm kind of relieved when he starts talking about unimportant stuff, like the weather and the flood. He's doing most of the talking. I'm waiting for the right opportunity to ask him about Charity.

He starts talking about his family, and I'm hanging on his every word, hoping he'll mention his ex-girlfriend.

He breaks his Pop-Tart in half and stares at the red filling for a beat. "My sister passed away recently." He lets that sentence hang there as a pained expression crosses his face.

"I'm so sorry."

Perry's focus leaves his Pop-Tart and shifts to me. The whites in his eyes have turned pink. "Thank you."

He gets up to grab another log, bare feet walking slowly, being careful where he steps. Sparks fly into the air when he drops the log onto the fire. "I just love a good fire. Don't you love the smell?" He takes a deep breath through his nose.

"Yeah, I guess so."

I think it's time for me to be brave and ask him about Charity, before he brings up another sad topic, although I don't think he could possibly bring up anything worse than losing his sister.

Perry pours another cup of hot chocolate and offers me a refill. "No. I'm good," I say.

I ball up my empty wrapper, stuff it into my pocket, and take a deep breath. Just ask him. Get it over with, I tell myself. "So I saw you yesterday in town. I was at the diner. Jesse's Diner." Perry doesn't seem fazed by my mentioning this. He's chowing down on Pop-Tarts, sipping his hot chocolate, just like he was before. "Anyway, I was wondering if you know one of the waitresses there. Her name is Charity."

He squints his eyes like he's trying to remember. "Oh yeah. The girl with the long black hair." He chuckles like he thinks this is funny for some reason. "She was my waitress. I ordered the waffles. Have you tried them?" Perry looks at me from over the top of his mug as he takes another drink of hot chocolate.

Stay on the subject. "Do you know Charity?" I ask again. "Are you two friends?"

"I asked her out, but she turned me down."

I'm stunned at his answer. Is he being serious? Did he really ask her out? Does he really not know her?

"That girl is smoking hot." He arches an eyebrow, looking at me. "So are you."

I feel the hair on the back of my neck stand up. I hope he doesn't think I'm here to flirt with him. Oh gosh. That is what he thinks. Of course it is. I showed up here, didn't I? I just walked right up to him by myself. What else is he going to think? I need to end this. "I've got a boyfriend."

Perry smiles, which I interpret to mean that he doesn't care. Now I'm even more concerned. I have a really bad feeling about him. The only reason I've stayed this long is because I want to find out about Charity. But this is getting too creepy.

He tosses the extra hot chocolate from his mug onto the ground. Gets up and walks over to his shoes and socks to check if they're dry.

"Well, I've gotta go." I spring to my feet and start toward the trees. "Thanks for breakfast."

"Hey."

My pace quickens, and I don't turn back.

"I was hoping we could hang out some more," he calls.

I don't answer. I keep moving, hoping I won't hear footsteps or heavy breathing behind me.

CHAPTER 41

ROY

I'm about to turn back and hike up the hill when I hear someone calling my name. The voice—I recognize it instantly. Relief swells inside me as I turn around. It's Samantha! I can't believe it. But there she is, stumbling down the trail toward me. She breaks into a run. She's still half a football field away, but I can tell she is smiling from ear to ear. I am too.

I race to close the distance between us. We collide, and I scoop her into my arms, picking her up off the ground. "I was so worried about you." We squeeze each other tightly as if we haven't seen each other in years. I set her down and slide my hand up the back of her neck, fingers tangling in her soft hair. I tilt her head back and press my lips against hers, and I know I never want to be with anyone else.

When we pull apart, she gasps for air, trying to catch her breath.

I hold her face in my hands, studying her, unsure what she has been through or where she has been, hoping she's okay. "Are you all right?"

She points over her shoulder. "The road flooded over, so I had to stay the night at the campground. I wanted to call you to tell you, but my cell phone isn't working."

"I know. All the phones are down."

I tuck a strand of her hair behind her ear, staring into her beautifully mismatched eyes, grateful she's safe. Then I hug her again. "I missed you so much."

"I missed you too, and I didn't mean to worry you. I thought I would make it back in time."

"So tell me what happened."

She sits down on a large rock and tells me about how she followed a guy named Perry. She suspected he might be Charity's ex-boyfriend. "I thought for sure he had tracked her down and was going to hurt her or maybe kidnap her."

I don't understand why Samantha was so concerned about Charity's safety. I was under the impression that she didn't even like Charity. I guess I was wrong, but still, it bothers me that she put herself in danger. "You followed him?" A tear rolls down her cheek, and I take hold of her hand. "What is it? What happened?" The thought crosses my mind that maybe we're not alone. I look over my shoulder and check the path behind me.

Samantha takes a deep breath, trying to compose herself. "It's just been a long night…and morning." She wipes her face with the sleeve of her coat.

I'm rubbing her hand, wishing I could do more to comfort her. "Samantha."

She pulls her hand away and more tears roll down her cheeks.

"Did something happen to you?" My mind jams with all of the possibilities, none of them good.

She shakes her head, wiping her face again. "No. It's not that." She sniffs. "It's us."

"Us?" Is she going to tell me about Spike? Is she going to break up with me now? Here?

"You're cheating on me with *Charity*. Aren't you?"

I'm stunned by her accusation. I haven't done anything inappropriate with Charity, but then why do I feel guilty? I have noticed how beautiful Charity is and wondered what life would be like if we were together. But I didn't allow myself to act on those thoughts. I have remained faithful to Samantha. "I haven't cheated on you."

Her lips twist. "Someone sent me a picture of you and Charity together. How do you explain that?"

She received a picture too? Someone is deliberately trying to break us up. Who would do that? "What do you mean, *together*?"

The tears keep coming. "I would show it to you but the battery on my phone is dead. You were cheek to cheek, practically lip to lip! Have you kissed her? Have you—"

"No, I'm not cheating on you," I interrupt her, hoping that she will calm down and listen. In no way does a picture like that exist, unless someone faked it. "I never kissed Charity. Please believe me."

Samantha's brows knit together. "I've seen the way you look at her, the way you act whenever she's around, how you flirt with her…" Samantha's list of incriminating evidence, all of her scrutinizing observations and her interpretations of every word I have ever uttered, every smile I allowed to appear on my face—it is all being twisted and turned into something more than it really is. Her face is red, her voice is raised.

I can't sit here and keep listening to this. I haven't slept, I haven't eaten. I had been so afraid that I might have shot and killed her. And now I'm worried about Grandma—afraid I might never see her again. I've got the hotel to run and all of those people staying there. I can't call the police, and even if I could they wouldn't be able to come and search for her. The roads are flooded. The one girl who I thought I could rely on is screaming at me, and I'm about at my own breaking point.

"Listen to me. I can't do this right now." I raise my voice and Samantha finally stops talking. "My grandma is missing. Nobody knows where she is. I've been wandering around these woods looking for you both since last night. We found her flashlight near a creek that has turned into a raging river. It's possible that she fell into the freezing water. The chances of her surviving are slim to none. But I'm holding out hope; maybe because I'm desperate, maybe because I'm delusional, but I'm hoping against all odds that maybe she's still out here somewhere, alive, and she needs my help."

I shake my head, wondering if I should continue. "I wasn't going to tell you this, Samantha, but I guess I have to now. You're not the only one who received a scandalous picture. Someone sent me a picture of you and Spike. So tell me, Samantha, are you cheating on me?"

I wait a couple beats for her to answer but she doesn't. "How does it feel to be accused of something you didn't do? Huh? I wish you would just have some faith and trust me. Because if there was ever a time that I needed you, the time is now. My mom is gone, my grandfather is gone, and now my grandmother. I'm the only one left in my family. Everybody has been taken from me!"

Samantha is sobbing, shoulders hunched forward, hands over her face. Now I'm feeling even worse. I've just yelled at the girl I love. I turn and walk away so I don't have to see how hurt she is. I never wanted to be the reason she cried. She deserves better than that. She deserves better than me.

CHAPTER 42

CHARITY (BELLANY)

As I walk down these winding, hilly trails, following behind Spike and Tracy, my mind hovers over what happened back at the hotel.

Pam and Todd are going to be starting over somewhere, possibly taking on new identities. I know exactly what that's like. I felt like I was reborn when I arrived here in Chehalis. A new name, a new identity, new friends.

I amaze myself at how quickly I've managed to turn things around in my favor here. It's been less than two months, and I've almost reached my goal. Veronica is gone. Samantha is gone. Roy is most definitely falling in love with me. When we get married, his inherited fortune will be mine.

Tracy turns to check and see if I'm keeping up. She takes the opportunity to glare at me for the hundredth time. When her head is turned back around I stick my tongue out at her.

Spike turns around next. "Hanging in there?" he asks.

"How much longer until we get to the campsite?"

He motions like he wants me to climb on his back. "Want me to carry you?" he grins.

Tracy whips around, mouth agape. "You are not going to carry her! She has two legs. She can walk on her own."

Spike makes a face at me. "See what I have to put up with?"

I smile at him as if I'm amused. The bottom of my foot is killing me. I think I'm getting a blister. I actually would like him to carry me.

"Look!" Spike points. "There it is."

Through a break in the trees I can see tents and cars. Finally! So now what? Are we going to wander around for another hour in search of Samantha? I'm only interested in finding Roy.

As our feet hit the dirt road, Tracy starts waving at a short man, probably in his forties, decked out in camouflage.

Spike gives him a fist bump. "Yo, Mr. Iverson. How goes it?"

Suddenly this trip has become interesting again. I finally get to meet Joshua Iverson, the lucky recipient of a whopping five hundred dollars a month from dear old Veronica. I can't wait to bring up her name and see how he reacts.

CHAPTER 43

SAMANTHA

I want to follow after Roy. I should have done it the second he left, but I hesitated. Now he's long gone. Even if I find him, I'm not sure he will want to talk to me. I have never heard him raise his voice or seen him lose his temper like he did. I had no idea that Veronica was missing. Why didn't he tell me that from the start? If he had, I would never have brought up that whole cheating thing. Talk about the absolute worst timing. I feel like such an idiot.

A rustling in the bushes snaps me from my thoughts. Did he come back?

I wipe the tears from my face, peering through the trees as the figure approaches. My stomach dips when I see who it is: the beard, the dark eyes, the baseball cap. What is he doing here?

"Perry?" I gasp, rising to my feet. Suddenly I'm aware of just how vulnerable I am out here. The feeling inside my gut is like I'm falling from the sky and my parachute won't open. I'm full of dread. I know something's wrong. His eyes; they're different. The light inside them is gone. Is he mad at me for taking off so suddenly? Why is he looking at me like that?

He raises his hand, pointing a knife directly at me. My chest constricts, heart hammering against my rib cage. "I've been looking for you," he sneers.

"What?" I gasp. "Why were you looking for me? I didn't do anything to you."

"True, but that doesn't matter. This isn't personal. You're just in the way, and it's my job to remove you."

Remove me? "How am I in the way—in the way of what?"

"I can't have you interfering with Roy and Charity." He cocks his head, eyes boring through me.

I swallow hard. "What are you talking about?"

Perry scrunches his face and squints for a few seconds. "I guess it's all right if you know why you have to go. The dead tell no tales… right?"

My feet don't move, but I'm scanning my surroundings, wondering if there's some way for me to escape.

"See, it's like this. Now that Veronica is dead, ol' Roy Boy is about to inherit everything. And once he and Charity get together, she'll be a beneficiary too. I can't have you getting in the way of that."

Is Veronica really dead? Is he sure? Did he…kill her? I'm freaking out. "I don't know anything about any inheritance, but if Charity is paying you to come after me, I'm sure Roy will pay you double if you just leave us alone."

"Sorry, but I'm not here to negotiate with you." He takes another step toward me. "I wanted to do this last night while you were asleep in the tent, but Mack stayed up too late, so I had to wait." His eyes narrow. "This is a much better spot anyway—much more private."

Perry is way bigger than me. He looks strong, athletic, fully capable of doing what he is threatening. My body wants to run, flee, escape. All of my muscles are tense, ready to go. But my mind is telling me not to do it. I won't be able to get away from him. He'll catch me. I've got to try something else. Maybe I can convince him not to do this. Maybe he'll change his mind. "But I thought you were after Charity."

"Why would I want to hurt the girl that I love?" The wind picks up. Branches and leaves recoil from a sharp gust, carrying Perry's menacing laugh through the air.

An overwhelming sense of finality sinks in, and I almost can't breathe. He's not after her? "I thought you wanted revenge, because she left you. She said she escaped from you—that you were abusive— that you tried to kill her—"

Perry nods with a smug look on his face. "That's exactly what you were supposed to think."

I swallow hard, desperate to think of something to say. He takes a step closer, and I move a step back, my eyes trained on his knife, waiting for him to strike—hoping I'll be able to fight him off.

He points the knife at my throat. "Charity and I have a long history together. She is still my girlfriend. We never broke up."

"Does she know that?" I ask, my voice shaking. "I mean, what about Roy?"

He shakes his head. "Charity isn't who you think she is. She doesn't love Roy. She loves me. Her real name is Bellany. And my name isn't Perry. That's the last name of the girl that she killed. My name is Quentin. I'm her boyfriend."

"Sh-she killed someone?" I stutter, my mind whirling with all of this new information. I still don't understand what's going on. "So you two are still together, and you go around looking for complete strangers…to befriend them…with all these complicated lies…just to murder them? Why?"

"It's been our plan all along to swindle Roy out of his inheritance. But in order to do that, we realized that we needed to get rid of Veronica and you. With you two out of the way, Charity can continue to manipulate and control Roy. He'll think he's falling in love with her, but he'll be falling in love with a lie. Sooner or later, he'll meet the same fate as you."

The wind, the rustling trees, everything around me all seems to go silent. He steps forward again, and I mirror his movement, taking a step back. His legs are so long, his arms too. There's no way I can outrun him.

I've got to convince him not to do this. I've got to change his mind somehow. "You think she won't turn on you?" I ask. "You actually think she'll want to be with you, when she can have Roy?"

"What's that supposed to mean?" his voice rises. "You think I'm not good enough? You think Roy is better than me? A country hick like him?" Perry looks me up and down with a disgusted expression on his face. "You don't know anything."

"I wasn't trying to insult you—I swear I wasn't. I just mean that she's spending all this time with him. Aren't you afraid she's going to fall in love with him for real? I mean, you're okay with her being with him: kissing him, holding him, touching—"

"Shut up!" he yells, lunging forward. I wrinkle my eyes shut, holding my breath, waiting for the pain to hit. Fingers grab hold of my arm, digging into my flesh, and my eyes pop back open from the pain. He raises the knife in the air, and I wish I hadn't looked—I don't want to see it coming. I squeeze my eyes shut again, waiting for death to come and take me. Please be quick, I think to myself. Please don't make me suffer.

The sound of brush rustling and twigs cracking nearby distracts Quentin. We both whip our heads in the direction of the noise. I don't see anything, but I know this is my moment. If I don't try to get away now, I will die here.

CHAPTER 44

ROY

I'm still pointing the gun, arms extended, holding my breath and aiming at a target that's no longer there. My line of sight tells me exactly what happened… The target is down.

I was shooting to kill—two rapid deliberate shots. The echo ricochets through the trees like thunder. A high-pitched ringing lingers in my ears.

Samantha is crumpled on the ground sobbing, her hands covering her face.

With the gun still in my hand, I stand over the stranger. His blue jacket is turning black in the center of his chest. A separate pool of blood soaks the ground around his head. I see an entrance wound above his left eye. I don't even have to nudge him to know that he's dead.

I crouch down beside Samantha and brush her hair out of her face. She looks up at me, eyes wide, still full of terror. Specks of red dot the side of her face and hair.

"Are you okay?" I ask, looking her over to make sure she isn't hurt. I had seen the knife in the stranger's hand, but it doesn't look like he had a chance to use it.

"I…I think so," Samantha's voice breaks, and she starts crying.

I gently reach around her shoulder, pulling her into my chest. We stay this way; not moving, not letting go, holding each other. When she finally pulls away, she's looking down at my hand. I didn't realize I was still holding the gun.

"That's my dad's gun," she says.

"I found it in your hotel room."

"I'm so glad you found it and that you brought it. Otherwise, I'd probably be dead right now." She looks over at the body. "You saved my life."

I notice the blood spatter on her face again. Some of it has transferred onto my hands. "What happened? Who was that guy?"

"You're never going to believe this—"

Voices fill the air. Samantha's face hardens and she instantly goes silent. I turn to see Spike, Tracy, Mr. Iverson, and Charity all coming toward us.

I'm about to stand up when Samantha snatches the gun out of my hand. "Samantha," I say in a low, calm voice. "What are you doing? That trigger is very sensitive."

She widens her stance, raising the gun and holding it steady, eyes fixed. She could hit any one of them.

"Samantha, stop. Give me the gun," I say, calmly.

She doesn't blink, doesn't move. Her focus is solely on her target.

"Charity!" she yells.

Spike and Tracy bail out of the way. Charity slips behind Mr. Iverson, who's standing there with his hands raised in the air. In one swift movement she whips out a switchblade and holds it against his throat. Mr. Iverson isn't much taller than she is, but he is twice as wide. She's using him as a human shield.

"Get away from him!" Samantha shouts, the gun still poised at the ready.

"What's going on?" Tracy cries.

Samantha glares at Charity. "I know what you've been up to. I know everything."

"Yo, there's a dead body over here," Spike says, pointing.

"Roy," Samantha says, "they killed Veronica, and I was gonna be next. They were trying to get your inheritance."

She's dead? The hope I had been clinging to vanishes as I realize my grandma is really gone. A torrential mix of anguish, guilt, and rage comes crushing down on me.

"Did you shoot him, Samantha?" Spike asks.

I look at the body and then at Charity. My head is spinning. How could I have been so trusting? So naive?

"His name's Quentin," Samantha says. "He was Charity's boyfriend."

I expect to see some kind of reaction from Charity, but she doesn't move or speak at all. She doesn't look scared either. I guess I shouldn't be surprised. She's a sociopath; I know this now. She doesn't have a conscience, and I truly believe she'll use that knife. She doesn't care about any of us. We're all just tools to her.

"Roy!" Mr. Iverson shouts, panic thick in his voice. "Make that girl lower her gun. You make her put it down, you hear!" His eyes appear twice their normal size. The desperate expression on his face makes me feel guilty, not just for what's happening now, but for everything that happened in the past.

I carefully hold my hand out to Samantha, staring directly at her, hoping she'll snap out of it and listen to me. If she's not careful, she'll end up killing Mr. Iverson. "Lower the gun, take your finger off of the trigger, and give it to me."

"She doesn't deserve to live."

"I know you're upset—I am too. Let's just handle this in a different way. Okay? Give me the gun."

"No!" Samantha's scream echoes in the air. Mr. Iverson's face contorts with fear, but Charity doesn't even flinch.

If I forcibly try to take the gun from her, it will almost certainly go off. All I can do is talk to her and hope that she will listen. "Please be careful," I say in a calm voice. "You don't want to hurt Mr. Iverson."

Samantha's brows draw down, her eyes fixed on Charity. "What is she saying to him? She's whispering something in his ear. Stop it!"

Charity's mouth is barely moving, her voice so low I can't hear what she's saying either. But judging by Mr. Iverson's terrified expression, he can hear her loud and clear. I know it's dangerous to wait around for Charity to make the next move, and I have no idea what she's up to. I feel powerless; I know I can't stop her. The only thing I can do is try to keep Samantha from making a mistake she'll regret for the rest of her life.

"Roy," Mr. Iverson says with a shaky voice. "Take that gun from her before she blows my head off. Don't just stand there. Do something. You owe me this much, Roy. I'm begging you. Don't let her take my life, like you took my boy's life. Liam didn't deserve to die, and neither do I."

My stomach drops when I hear him mention Liam's name. He knows what happened? When did he find out? All this time, I thought it was just Grandma and I who knew the truth.

Samantha glances at me, and I nod. "He's right. Please. Give me the gun, and I'll explain." If telling the truth will get Samantha to lower the gun, then I'll do it. Even if that means I have to go to jail for what I've done, at least then I would be the one getting locked up and not Samantha. I can't let her risk ruining her entire life in an act of stupid revenge. I'm the one who deserves to be punished. I should have told the truth a long time ago. Keeping this secret has slowly eaten away at my soul.

Samantha lowers the gun to her side, but her eyes remain fixed on Charity.

I take a slow step closer to her. "I know you want Charity to suffer for what she's done. So do I. But you can't do this. There's a right way to handle things, and this isn't it."

"Charity deserves to die," Samantha says through gritted teeth.

"Please," Mr. Iverson calls. "Put the gun down."

Samantha's eyes slide over to mine, and she stares at me.

"Samantha, I love you. I don't want to be apart from you—not ever." This is the first time I've told her that I love her, and I'm not saying it to manipulate her. I mean it. She's my world, my universe. She means everything to me.

The crease between her eyebrows disappears and a tear slides down her cheek. "I love you too."

I slowly remove the gun from her fingers and whisper, "I mean it. I really do love you, Samantha."

"Roy," Charity shouts. "You need to lose the gun. Throw it into the woods, and I don't mean just toss it. I want you to throw it as far as you can. I swear, if you don't, I'll slit his throat." Mr. Iverson's neck is already dripping with blood. She's got the knife pressed way too hard against his skin. I don't doubt she'll kill him.

Spike and Tracy both give me a nod. I don't need their approval; I already know what I'm going to do.

The situation isn't fair, but I can't change it. All I can do is try to affect the outcome. Mr. Iverson's life is in danger, and I can't sacrifice him in an act of selfish revenge. There's been enough death already.

I cock my arm back and throw the gun into the trees as far as I can. What happens next is up to Charity.

"All of you," Charity shouts, "take your shoelaces out of your shoes and tie up each other's hands behind your backs."

"We're not going to do that," I tell her. "Look, you got what you wanted. Now let Mr. Iverson go."

"I'm not going to let him go until you're all tied up." Blood is rolling down his neck and onto her hand.

"But once we're tied up, what's to stop you from slitting our throats?" Samantha asks.

"I'm not going to hurt you if you do what I say. I just need to get out of here without you following me. So either do what you're told or you'll force me to take things in a direction you'll regret."

Charity has already proven that she can't be trusted. Whether she's being honest right now, I have no idea. But I feel like we don't have another choice.

Tracy clears her throat, an expression of terror on her face. "How are we going to tie each other's hands? There's going to be one person without their hands tied."

"Tracy, you'll be the last one. Now shut up and do it!" Charity shouts. "Hurry up!"

Spike turns to me, a questioning look on his face. Charity is too far away for us to rush her.

"Do it now," Charity demands. "And then lie on the ground, face down."

"Everyone do it," I say, figuring that I'll be able to break free from a shoelace restraint if it comes to it.

With everyone's hands tied up, except for Tracy's, we kneel down and fall forward onto our stomachs.

"Tracy," Charity shouts, "bring your shoelaces and come over here so Mr. Iverson can tie your hands together."

There's silence for a few minutes while Tracy's hands are being tied.

"Now lie face down on the ground like the others," Charity says. "All of you, start counting to a thousand—out loud. If I hear that you've stopped, I'll slit his throat. Understand?"

Tracy is the first one to start counting, then the rest of us join in.

"Louder!" Charity demands, and we comply.

Spike's lying right next to me, his face turned toward Samantha. I wish I could see her, but I can't; he's in the way. I can only hear her voice, and that's just not enough. I want to be next to her, to touch her, to look into her eyes. Never again do I want to be without her. When that knife was about to end her life, I felt like my life would end too.

"Keep moving, fatso," I hear Charity say to Mr. Iverson as she leads him away. The sound of their footsteps begins to trail off.

When faced with the prospect of death, it's amazing how perspective shifts and the things that are truly important become crystal clear. I can see clearly now. I don't care if Samantha cheated on me with Spike; it doesn't matter. She loves me, and I love her. Things are going to be different between us—they're going to be much better. That's a promise I plan to keep.

My hands are almost free. I can feel the laces loosening as I continue to pull and twist. Finally there's a snap. I rush straight to Samantha next, untie her hands, then we both quickly untie Tracy and Spike.

"Let's go get her," I say, starting to run.

It's not easy traversing these trails at such a fast pace. It takes a lot of focus and concentration not to trip and fall, especially since our shoes don't have any laces in them.

"Hey," I call out for everybody to hear. "Once we spot them, we need to stay hidden. We can't let Charity know we're following her."

"That's right," Samantha agrees. "The element of surprise is crucial. I don't want this witch to get away again."

"I'm gonna kill her," Spike huffs, and he sounds like he means it. "I can't wait till I get my hands on her."

Tracy's quick to chastise him. "Don't you go doing anything stupid. I don't want to have to come and visit you in prison."

Soon Spike is so far ahead of us we can't see him anymore. Tracy tries to call him back, but he doesn't listen.

Once we make it over the next hill, we finally see him in the distance. He's no longer running. He's crouched down, looking at something.

Fearing the worst, I speed up until I see what he's staring at.

Blood is everywhere: It's on Spike's hands, on his shirt. But it isn't coming from him; he isn't injured. It's coming from Mr. Iverson. And Charity is nowhere in sight.

CHAPTER 45

CHARITY (BELLANY)

'm careful to remain hidden in the trees after leaving Mr. Iverson behind, and I make it to the campground without any problems. He was slowing me down, not cooperating, and really being a pain. I didn't have much of a choice in the matter; I had to take care of him. And really, he should thank me for being so gracious to him. I could have killed him if I wanted to, but instead I just gave him a few scars to remember me by. I'm sure he'll survive.

My heart is thrumming in my chest from running so fast and for so long. I feel like I'm almost out of breath, but I'm sure I can make it the rest of the way. I know I'm getting close. The water is just around the bend. I can hear it now.

I bet Roy and the rest of them think they're going to catch me, which is laughable—bunch of idiots. They underestimate me.

Earlier, when I came to the campsite with Tracy and Spike, I noticed some thoughtful campers brought kayaks with them. I saw them sitting at the edge of a swollen creek, ready and waiting for me, like a gift. The only thing that's missing is the bow on top.

Soon I catch sight of a bright yellow kayak, mixed in with the green grass, and a smile spreads across my face. There you are, sunshine.

I've never kayaked before, but I doubt it will be that hard to learn. All you have to do is paddle, right? Even a moron could do it.

I grab hold of the edge of the kayak and start pulling it toward the water. It's a lot heavier than I anticipated, but still, I can't complain. I don't have to pull it that far.

Rocks and sticks scrape along the bottom, like fingernails on a chalkboard. My feet sink into the muddy ground with each step I take. This would be so much easier if I had a partner.

Most of the kayak is in the water now. It's unstable due to the swift current, but the rest of this should be easy. I just need to stay dry and not fall in. I turn to position myself, ready to jump inside, and then I hear someone calling my name. I recognize the voice immediately. It's Roy. I don't want to look at him. I know it would do me no good to see his face: the expression of betrayal, devastation, pain, and whatever else he's feeling. I don't need or want to remember him that way. Nor do I want to dwell on what I've done. I'm just going to ignore that he's there.

I'm paddling quickly, my heart racing. The water ripples around me, crashing onto the surrounding rocks and trees. For a while, it seems like I can still hear someone calling me like an echo on constant repeat. But eventually the voice starts to fade, and soon I don't hear it anymore. I barely need to paddle. The river continues to carry me farther and farther away.

I think about the opportunity I've lost with Roy and his inheritance. Even worse, I've lost Quentin too. It seems so strange to be leaving him behind.

I never thought that he would end up getting killed like that. He seemed almost indestructible, especially since he had survived that blow to the head I had given him. I remember thinking that I had killed him. He wasn't breathing, and he wasn't moving. Then he gasped and took a deep breath, opening his eyes.

He knew he deserved it, because of what he had done to me. Later he said, "Your plans are my plans. I promise I will never hurt you again, and I swear I will never leave you."

I didn't believe him, but I held him to his word, even though he tried to go back on it when he heard about my plans with Roy. He didn't like the idea of me being with another guy. I told him that it would just be for a couple of months, and then we would get rid of Roy and be together again. I was lying when I said that to him, but he didn't know that. I had already made up my mind that I was going to be with Roy instead of Quentin. Roy was a better partner for me. For one thing, Roy wasn't an abuser. Quentin was, and he was becoming more and more like my father every day.

I decided that after I had finished using Quentin I was going to get rid of him for good. But just like Veronica, it turned out that

I didn't have to actually do anything. They both ended up getting killed on their own.

I let out a deep breath, relaxing my shoulders. As I look up at the sky, I see the clouds part and bright sunlight pouring through—a rare sight around here. The floodwaters will be receding soon, and the roads will clear. Life will go on, for those who haven't died yet. I'll never return to Chehalis, Washington, nor will I go back to where I'm originally from, Smithfield, North Carolina. Those two places don't exist to me anymore. And that's not the only thing I'm erasing from my mind...

Goodbye, Charity.

Goodbye, Bellany.

Hello to a new me, a new life, a new future, and a new name. I smile, envisioning how I'll introduce myself to people: *Hello, my name is Tamara. It's nice to meet you.*

CHAPTER 46

SAMANTHA

The floodwaters have finally receded enough for most people to return to their houses. Dad should be arriving here sometime later today. The cops are searching for Charity. They're supposed to pick up Perry's dead body today. It's still lying in the same spot, in the middle of the woods.

Roy seems to be doing okay, considering he's lost his grandmother. We figure she must have drowned in the flood and hope her body will be located soon.

Things with me and Spike are over. He was surprisingly decent when I had the conversation with him. I think everything we've been through these past few days has really been a humbling experience for everyone.

Roy told us what happened to Mr. Iverson's son. He said, "The last time it flooded, five years ago, after all of the hotel guests were checked in, my grandma and I had some extra time on our hands. So we decided to head to the back of the property with our rifles to do some target practice. We used to do this all the time. Mostly, I would do it with my grandfather, but he wasn't feeling well, so he stayed behind at the hotel to cover the office... It was my turn to shoot. I had a target set up about fifty yards away. It was a tin can sitting on a pile of wood. My finger was poised on the trigger, and I was already pulling when I saw Liam come out of nowhere, running right in front of it."

Roy said his grandparents never told him what happened to Liam's body. They said it was in everyone's best interest that they never speak about it again. As a thirteen-year-old who had recently lost his mom, he did what they told him and buried his emotions down deep.

After all the recent murders, and everything that happened with Charity and Quentin, he's only now coming to terms with these past traumas.

Roy is sitting next to me with Roscoe on his lap. We're down to just a few remaining hotel guests. More check out every day.

A guy wearing a cowboy hat enters the lobby and approaches the counter. I move my hands to the keyboard, ready to enter his name. He doesn't plan on checking out yet, he informs us, and wants to stay a couple extra days. Then he asks for Charity, and my stomach does a weird flippy thing. Both Roy and I look at each other at the exact same time. Then Roy sets Roscoe down on the floor and stands up. "You're CJ, right?"

"That's right," he replies. "You remembered."

"Why do you want to talk to Charity?" I ask him.

He leans onto the counter, and I get the impression this answer isn't going to be quick. He has a story to tell. "I host a podcast called *Unsolved, Unfinished: Criminals on the Run*. Have you heard of it?"

I shake my head.

"On my podcast, I refer to myself as Cam. But I also go by CJ."

Roy and I exchange looks again. I don't know what this guy wants. There are a lot of people with podcasts.

He cocks his head, eyes gleaming like he's ready to let us in on a big secret. "I've been investigating the disappearance of Bellany Silverfield, who you both know as Charity. It wasn't easy to track her down, believe me. Is she still here?" He searches our eyes, then exhales a deep breath. "Please don't tell me she's taken off again."

From the corner of my eye, I can see Roy's back stiffen.

Roy told me how he had chased after Charity. The river carried her kayak farther and farther away from him as he ran along the bank, dodging trees, rocks, whatever got in his way. He was unable to stop her, and he's still mad at himself for letting that happen. I told him it wasn't his fault. I think it's just going to take some time for him to get over it. I place my hand on his arm to help calm him down.

"Charity isn't here," I say. "She's run off, and we don't know where she is."

CJ covers his mouth, defeat written all over his face. He should know by looking at us that we feel the same. Charity has turned our lives upside down. She murdered Roy's grandmother, tried to have me killed, and was planning on eventually killing Roy too.

CJ removes his hat and rakes his hand through his hair. "I have been tracking her down for three months, following up on leads, spending all of my money. Then I caught a break. A truck driver gave me a tip that panned out, bringing me here. I tried calling the cops but the cell signal was down and they couldn't get here anyway, so…" He shrugs. "I have been keeping an eye out for her around the hotel and hadn't seen her. Now I know why."

Roscoe is whining at my feet, so I bend down to pick him up.

"I got something to show you." CJ reaches inside his bag and pulls out a laptop, setting it down on the counter in front of us. "This is Bellany's, or Charity's, whatever you want to call her. I broke into her room and stole it. It took me a couple days to hack the password, but I finally got it. From what I've seen on here, it looks like she's been messing with you two. You should look at the photos she created."

The computer beeps as it powers up. While it continues to load, CJ hands me his business card. "You two should be guests on my podcast. Sounds like you have a lot you could add."

While Roy and I are looking at the photos on the laptop, CJ tells us all about Bellany and how she's on the run from the police, which is how she ended up here.

I interrupt his story to inform him that Roy shot and killed Quentin. This bit of news rendered CJ speechless and took him some time to process. "Where is he at?" he asks.

Roy nods toward the trails. "His body is still out there in the woods."

CJ strokes his chin, thinking. "Do you mind if I go check it out? I'll be sure not to touch anything. I promise."

"Yeah, whatever," Roy replies.

"But just don't expect us to go with you," I add.

When CJ leaves, we cue up his podcast. By the time he returns, Roy decides to offer him some money to continue his investigation. CJ gladly and graciously accepts the money and decides not to extend his stay after all. He wants to get started tracking Charity down right away, and I'm all too eager for him to do it.

Part of me wishes I could go with him. I bet Roy feels the same way. But we have to stay here and finish high school.

Before CJ leaves, he turns back to us and says, "Don't worry, I'll find her. I've done it once. I can do it again."

It's a nice thought. I hope he does manage to find her. As he's about to leave, I feel like I need to warn him: "Be careful. And don't underestimate her." I feel extremely fortunate to still be alive and to be with Roy.

Dad and I stay at the hotel while our house is being repaired from the flood damage. We've been helping Roy run the hotel, sharing in all of the responsibilities, even the unpleasant jobs like cleaning.

"How bad was that last room?" Roy asks, knowing full well I'm at my wit's end.

I shake my head. "Believe me. You do not want to know."

"Okay, let's just hire someone to take care of stuff like that." He switches on the computer. As it's loading, he looks at me from over his shoulder. "What?"

I guess he noticed the anxious expression on my face. "Promise me one thing."

He turns, giving me his full attention. "Anything."

"I get to hire the next housekeeper." I smile, because I meant that as a joke.

He doesn't smile back at me. His expression is blank, and I don't know if I have upset him. Maybe I have. I'm about to look away when I see a smile slowly spread across his face.

For the first time in a long time, we both start to laugh. We laugh so hard and for so long that our stomachs start to ache and our eyes water. Roy tries to walk over to a chair and sit down, but he trips and almost falls. This only makes us laugh harder.

Sometimes shared traumatic experiences can bind people together, and sometimes they can tear them apart. For me and Roy, I feel like we've definitely grown closer. Our emotional wounds are still healing, but as a result, we're both going to be left with matching scars engraved on our souls forever.

READ ON FOR
A SNEAK PEEK AT THE
NEXT IN THE SERIES

CHAPTER 1

WINTER

Deaths always come in threes. People might call that an old saying or a superstition, but I believed it was true. Back in Utah, when my friend Venus Swensen was murdered by her ex-boyfriend, he also killed her younger brother and sister. Three dead. Here in North Carolina, there had already been two deaths: My Aunt Emma and her fiancé Reginald, which meant a third was coming, and soon.

Through the bug splattered windshield, my eyes traveled up the large staircase that led to the front door of Aunt Emma's house. This place was nothing like the boxy, stilted beach houses down the road or across the street. From where I sat, I couldn't even see the rooftop–it was so tall. Despite the fact that it was a hundred degrees outside today and probably a hundred and twenty inside the SUV, I felt a cold shiver snake down my spine as I thought about what had happened inside this house.

Mom grabbed my arm, smiling at me. "Winter, just look at how beautiful this place is. It's a mansion!" She squealed like a game show contestant who had just won a big prize.

I wished she would stop. I pulled away, refusing to celebrate with her in spite of what I was seeing.

Mom and I had inherited this house from Aunt Emma, and that was a huge game changer for us. The nicest place we had ever lived before was a single wide trailer with a hole in the living room floor that we covered up with a piece of plywood and a rug. (Yes, people tripped over it all the time.) Mom would likely spend the rest of her life here. Odds were, I would too. There was no going back to Utah. All I knew for certain was that I would be starting my senior year of high school here in the fall–an unfamiliar place with no friends.

"Beach life, here we come!" Mom cheered, tucking a strand of sandy blonde hair behind her ear. The bright sun reflected off of her silver hoop earring. She did her happy dance, bouncing around in her seat like she was a teenager, a forty-year-old teenager.

But I couldn't share her enthusiasm. I couldn't even crack a smile. "Yeah. Here's to beach life," I muttered. "Sun, surf, and suppressed emotions."

Mom shouldn't have been so happy. We had just picked up Aunt Emma's ashes from the funeral home. That was our first stop when we arrived in Kure Beach. What bothered me the most about Mom's behavior was that I felt like she was genuinely glad her sister had died. To say that Mom hated Aunt Emma wasn't a strong enough statement to describe how she really felt about her. The last time they spoke to each other was eight years ago, when I was ten.

The SUV's door squealed as I pushed it open and climbed out–the smell of the salty sea air quickly replacing the odor of greasy fast food wrappers and stale french fries. Mom started taking pictures of the house with her phone. I turned to look at the cardboard box sitting in the back seat that held Aunt Emma's ashes. *I'm sorry,* I thought to myself, wishing that she was still alive so she could hear me.

I wanted to hold a funeral service for Aunt Emma, but Mom was opposed to this idea. She argued that there weren't any other family members besides us to invite. Still, I thought we should do something, maybe have a minister perform a eulogy, and Mom and I would dress up in black. But pretending like Aunt Emma never existed and ignoring the fact that she died, only made me feel worse.

When we were at the funeral home, I begged Mom–once again–to hold a funeral service for her. Mom glared at me and said, "I highly doubt that your aunt had any friends to invite."

Like Mom had room to talk. She went through friends like tissues. But sadly, she was probably right. Aunt Emma tended to center her entire life around one person, and that one person was usually whoever she was dating or engaged to at the time. This last guy she was engaged to, Reginald Fontaine, must have expected that she would actually follow through and marry him, because he left her everything in his will. And when Aunt Emma died, she left everything to me and Mom. I had hoped Mom might feel at least a little gratitude and want to pay her respects, but even in death she couldn't find any respect for her sister.

I had never met Reginald, so I didn't know anything about him. Aunt Emma's estate attorney, Mr. Davis, told us that he passed away from a heart attack on April first. Yes, on April Fools' Day. Then Aunt Emma died on April thirteenth. Friday the thirteenth. Bad luck and irony. I wondered what might come next.

Mom started walking toward the house. Hopefully there wasn't a black cat about to cross our path.

"Wait," I said, pointing back to the SUV. "Don't forget the ashes."

"It'll be fine. We can get that later."

No, it won't be fine and you know it. "We can't leave Aunt Emma in here."

"Why not? It's not like it's gonna kill her. She's already dead."

"Mom!" I glared at her, horrified. I couldn't believe she said that out loud.

"You're always such a worrier, Winter. Trust me. It's fine." She waved me off like I was being ridiculous. As if abandoning a dead relative in the back seat was normal behavior.

I picked up the box that contained Aunt Emma's ashes, then caught up to Mom, walking past tall palm trees and flowering bushes. At the edge of the manicured front lawn I could see a path made of crushed shells and sand disappear around the corner of the house. The roar of ocean waves crashed in the distance. I guessed the path must lead to the beach. I continued up the front steps.

The sprawling porch and huge double doors made me feel like I was stepping into a fairytale. In spite of this being an older home, it appeared to be in pristine condition. The deep purple paint might have felt loud or tacky anywhere else, but here, against its crisp white trim it looked elegant. I felt the tension in my neck and shoulders start to relax. Something about the color purple has always had a calming effect on me. I loved it so much that I dyed the ends of my blonde hair purple, giving an ombre effect.

Mom reached inside her overflowing purse, fishing around for the house key. Unable to find it, she set her purse down on the welcome mat and began emptying everything out. "I can't wait to see what it looks like inside," she said as she peered up at me, grinning. "Winter, you're going to love it here—I just know you will. We were made for beach life."

As if saying the same thing over and over makes it true—but she couldn't have been more wrong. Maybe she was made for beach life, with her sun-kissed hair and perfect tan, but I wasn't. Not at all. Whenever I spent time in the sun, my skin started at white, then went straight to red, immediately followed by regret. I had been named *Winter*, the exact opposite of summer. Plus, I couldn't even swim. I did not belong here.

I leaned against the porch railing and turned my attention to the coral-colored house next door. With expansive balconies on its second and third floors, it was just as beautiful and grand as Aunt Emma's. A dune buggy with big bumpy wheels sat tucked inside the garage. I had to admit, that vehicle actually looked like a lot of fun. I wondered if Aunt Emma had one of those parked inside her garage too.

As my eyes continued to scan the house next door, I noticed a person's silhouette hovering in the upstairs window behind a sheer curtain. The dark shadow remained motionless, even though I was staring directly at it.

I turned my attention to Mom again. She was still searching for the house key.

Instead of taking in the rest of the view around me, my eyes focused on a single palm tree, not because I was admiring it. I was trying to act like nothing was wrong. But in truth, I was becoming increasingly anxious. I swear I could still feel that person in the window staring at us, just like I could feel the heat from the sun.

After several long seconds, maybe a minute, I turned and looked up at the window again. My stomach dipped. The shadow was still there. I immediately dropped my gaze as if I hadn't noticed, as if I wasn't extremely bothered by the fact that Mom and I were under surveillance by some stranger.

A normal person wouldn't stand there and stare like that, not unless they were trying to send a message like *I'm a pervert and I'm watching you*, or *I'm nosey and I'm judging you*, or *I'm a murderer and I'm going to kill you*. I didn't believe I was being paranoid to think these things. I was only being realistic. "Here we go!" Mom pulled out two house keys and slid one of them into the lock.

Before walking inside, I looked up at the window one last time—just as a hand appeared, parting the curtains. A cold sensation settled upon me like a storm cloud. Goosebumps raced down my arms. I could make out the outline of a person's shoulders, their neck, and a baseball cap on top of their head, but couldn't see a face. Whoever was staring at me wasn't just being a nosey neighbor. I could feel that this person was much worse—way more sinister. Darkness radiated from them. I could feel it all the way to my bones. No longer able to contain my fear, I turned and rushed inside the house, slamming the door behind me.

I stood there, my entire body tense, heart pounding rapidly, my hands clutching the box of Aunt Emma's ashes. Slowly the room started coming into focus. I felt as though I had been transported to another world and became fully engrossed in my surroundings. This was not what I expected. From the outside, this house looked like a vacation postcard with a brightly colored beach vibe, but inside there was no hint of the beach anywhere, not a single seashell, mermaid, or picture of the ocean.

Everywhere I looked something glistened and sparkled, catching the light from the sun shining through the windows. Crystal chandeliers hung from the ceiling. Glass sconces and mirrors adorned the walls. White marble tiles sprawled across the floors. The glass tables had even more glass on top of them: etched bowls, decorative lamps and vases. I was almost afraid to touch anything for fear that I might break it. Even the tiniest piece of broken glass could penetrate the skin and draw blood.

Mom looked around the living room, eyes wide, smile even wider. "Doesn't this place just take your breath away?" She spun around, her skirt flaring out like a flower in full bloom. "I feel like a princess in an ice castle."

Doesn't ice melt in the sun? I wanted to ask but I didn't.

Mom disappeared somewhere as I began exploring the rest of the first floor on my own. I discovered that each room was similar in style, with only a slight change in color: The living room was white, the dining room was off-white, the family room was beige, the kitchen was buttercream yellow, and the bathroom was ivory.

I set Aunt Emma's ashes down on the bookshelf in the living room right next to an intricately carved crystal vase. Out of all the shiny pieces in the room, this one caught my eye the most, probably because it had such a complex pattern etched into it and looked the most expensive.   I wondered if the rest of the house was decorated the same way. I sure hoped not.

The massive staircase leading upstairs was probably six feet wide from bottom to top. A crystal chandelier hung directly above it, resembling an upside down wedding cake with lots of layers. My fingers trailed along the glass banister's smooth surface, then suddenly I remembered what Mr. Davis had told us. He said that Aunt Emma fell on these stairs. She was still conscious enough to call 9-1-1, but by the time the ambulance arrived, she had already died from her injuries.   "Winter!" Mom called with urgency in her voice.

A rush of adrenaline swept through me, and I took off running to find her.

Mom was standing in the family room, looking out the sliding glass door. "There's something going on out there," she said as she slid the door open, letting in a waft of hot, humid air.

I followed her out to the back deck, amazed at the view laid out before my eyes. Seagulls hovered in the clear blue sky above. Just beyond the back fence, people and umbrellas dotted the billowy sand. The massive ocean dominating the scenery, stretching out as far as I could see. Fierce waves crashed, one after another, the noise a constant roar in my ears.

As I gazed upon the beautiful landscape, I noticed something unexpected. Further down the beach to my right, a crowd of people hovered behind a barrier consisting of orange caution cones and yellow police tape.   Mom started down the path toward the beach. "Let's go see what happened."

I almost followed her but thought better of it. There was something I needed to do first. "I'm going to go get my shoes. I'll meet you out there." I turned around to go back inside so I could make sure the front door was locked.

With my flip-flops on and two house keys in hand, I locked the back door and headed to the beach, curious about what was going on. I found Mom all the way at the front of the crowd of onlookers. "Excuse me," I said, wedging past the people around her.

As I stood next to her, my eyes widened in surprise. I was finally able to see what she and everybody else was staring at. The shape under the white sheet made it perfectly clear.

There was a dead body.

ACKNOWLEDGMENTS

To my husband, Ryan, thank you for making it possible for me to chase this dream. Your support, patience, and steady encouragement have meant everything on this journey.

Meg Gibbons, your guidance has made this process smoother and more rewarding than I could've hoped. Shannon Thompson, your expert insight strengthened this story. I'm so grateful. And to the amazing team at Sourcebooks, thank you for everything you do behind the scenes.

Denise, my beta reader and closest friend, thank you for your honesty, your brilliance, and for always being there when I needed a boost.

To my readers, your enthusiasm is the heartbeat of this journey. Thank you for coming along with me.

ABOUT THE AUTHOR

Michele Leathers spent five years in Lewis County, Washington, specifically in the Centralia-Chehalis area. While this story is entirely fictional, she actually lived through a flood there and draws many insights and ideas from her experiences during that time. Today, she enjoys family, writing, exploring true crime cases, reading psychological thrillers, and finding inspiration in the small, eerie moments of everyday life. Michele lives in the Southeast United States with her family and a growing collection of vintage ceramic pie keepers.

Follow her on

Facebook: facebook.com/MicheleLeathersAuthor

Instagram: @author_michele_leathers

sourcebooks fire

Home of the hottest trends in YA!

Visit us online and
sign up for our newsletter at
FIREreads.com

....

Follow
@sourcebooksfire
online